Remarks from th

"I come to stories for that human elen[...] that makes me, with all of my individu[...] less alone. These stories made me seen [...] [...] did so with such care and beauty, I am ever hopeful that art and literature still possess the capacity to slow time, to change a life."
　　　　　—Dantiel W. Moniz, 2023 judge and author of *Milk Blood Heat*

"These stories undid me, and then sewed me back together with such bright threads I can almost now see the future."
　　　　　—Sabrina Orah Mark, 2022 judge and author of *Happily*

"It seems impossible that such an anthology could be assembled from debuts, but it's not: it is just the good fortune of every reader who finds this collection and begins to track the writing of these talented emerging authors."
　　　　　—Emily Nemens, 2022 judge and author of *The Cactus League*

"These stunning debut stories have stuck with me long after our job as judges was finished. I still recall the beautiful images as well as the shocking ones, the clever and hilarious wordplay, gutting lines of dialogue, and characters whose stories break my heart, haunt me, or both. I applaud these writers for their boldness, their skill, and their fierce imaginations."　　　　　—Deesha Philyaw, 2022 judge and author of *The Secret Lives of Church Ladies*

"Judging the prize felt a little like getting back to my roots. It brought me back to that organic and creative place, of being exploratory and experimental. It was shocking to me not just how well written these stories were, but how powerfully the writers' essential selves were coming through."　　　　　—Nana Kwame Adjei-Brenyah, 2021 judge and author of *Chain-Gang All-Stars*

"All these stories were vast in what they were able to imagine and make believe on the page. I am so proud of these stories."
　　　　　—Kali Fajardo-Anstine, 2021 judge and author of *Woman of Light*

"Drawing on a range of forms and diversity of voices, these stories are vivid and emotionally complex—a celebration of the short story as a form."   —Beth Piatote, 2021 judge and author of *The Beadworkers*

"The short fiction I love best knows how to declare with beauty, 'I prefer not to.' It takes the page as a space to refuse what tends to be, unzipping barriers. This collection gathers stories from voices throwing rice at the moment the essential and the original meet."
            —Tracy O'Neill, 2020 judge and author of *Quotients*

"Your first published story never quite gives up its place in the mind. It was the first one *chosen*—hooray! And yet there is always the nagging doubt ('Is it actually good?') and here we are, celebrating, saying, 'Yes, yes, it is good, so so good!'"   —Deb Olin Unferth, 2020 judge
                                        and author of *Barn 8*

"The stories and writers here represent a wide range of voices at the levels of ethnicity, gender, and style. Many carry a very quiet confidence that is refreshing in our harried world." —Nafissa Thompson-Spires, 2020 judge and author of *Heads of the Colored People*

"I was really inspired by what I saw here—not just the beautiful weirdness of the writers and their work, but the fact that the stories were published. It made me feel so hopeful." —Carmen Maria Machado, 2019 judge and author of *In the Dream House*

"I am so wildly enthusiastic about what these writers are going to do next—and in reading this anthology, you get to say you've followed their entire career, from the very first short story on! You can't beat that."   —Alexandra Kleeman, 2018 judge and
                                        author of *Something New Under the Sun*

"The best stories are almost otherworldly in their dimensions, as if I have opened a small suitcase left on my front door, only to find three geese, a small child, a jewel thief, and her mother emerging. The

stories here delighted and surprised and moved me—I'm so very, very glad that I got to read them and that now you do too."
—Kelly Link, 2017 judge, 2018 MacArthur Fellow, and author of *White Cat, Black Dog*

"When I read I'm always (like it or not) guessing what's going to happen at the end of the line, the scene, on the plot level. The stories we chose were those that forced me, a relentless overthinker, to stop thinking."
—Marie-Helene Bertino, 2017 judge and author of *Parakeet*

"A lot of people talk about how so many short stories are becoming too workshopped, too MFA, too a certain kind of story. And I can say, after reading all the entries here, they are wrong. There are so many stories being told that are extraordinary and unexpected. I fretted over picking only twelve. But the stories that won were all stories that astounded us all."
—Nina McConigley, 2017 judge and author of *Cowboys and East Indians*

Praise for the Best Debut Short Stories Series

"A tantalizing glimpse of the work of tomorrow's literary luminaries."
—*Poets & Writers*

"Urgent fiction, from breakout talents."
—*Booklist*

"A fresh, delightful collection of short fiction that looks to our literary future with promise."
—Cade Johnson, *ZYZZYVA*

"A welcome addition to the run of established short story annuals, promising good work to come."
—*Kirkus Reviews*

"A useful resource for writers, since each story is introduced by the editors of the literary magazine who first published each work, discussing what captured their interest and what makes the story successful."
—Lyndsie Manusos, *Book Riot*

Judges

Venita Blackburn

Richard Chiem

Dantiel W. Moniz

CATAPULT
NEW YORK

BEST DEBUT SHORT STORIES

2023

The PEN America Dau Prize

Edited by Summer Farah and Sarah Lyn Rogers

BEST DEBUT SHORT STORIES 2023

First Catapult edition: 2023

Please see permissions on page 205 for individual credits.

ISBN: 978-1-64622-201-8

Library of Congress Control Number: 2021936334

Cover design by Nicole Caputo
Cover art by Sirin Thada
Book design by Laura Berry

Catapult
New York, NY
books.catapult.co

Printed in the United States of America

10 9 8 7 6 5 4 3 2 1

CONTENTS

INTRODUCTION

THERE'S A SURPRISING COHESION IN THIS YEAR'S anthology. As in all previous years, our 2023 judges—Venita Blackburn, Richard Chiem, and Dantiel W. Moniz—were urged to select exciting, engaging stories that moved them, with no special consideration for themes or topics that might go together. So there must be something in the air right now.

The stories collected here share a sense of immediacy and an emphasis on subjective experience—with a majority written in present tense and nearly all written in a first-person perspective. These stories are concerned with physical bodies and the thorniest stages of interpersonal relationships: reproduction, birth, death, uncovered secrets. Half reference fluorescence, drawing our attention to what's artificial. In this collection, the natural world promises—or threatens—to triumph over constructed things.

At the time of writing, it is May 2023. The atmosphere is increasingly authoritarian: an uptick in book bans, legislation overriding rights to bodily autonomy, wave after wave of morale-crushing layoffs that disempower workers as corporations favor shareholders. And while so many populations fight for basic rights, creatives are faced with the proposition that our livelihoods could be replaced by AI. Twitter and Instagram are flooded with generative-AI images and texts that users say are created all in fun, but artists like Molly Crabapple are raising the alarm. In a recent panel at this year's International Journalism Festival, Crabapple asserted that the purpose of these generators, which were trained on stolen, copyrighted materials, is to "eliminate the need to pay" creatives. The Writers Guild of America went on strike last night; AI regulation was among the WGA's proposals that the Alliance of Motion Picture and Television Producers rejected outright: "Regulate use of artificial intelligence on MBA [Minimum Basic Agreement]-covered projects: AI can't write or rewrite literary material; can't be used as source material; and MBA-covered material can't be used to train AI." Corporate greed is nothing new, but what's bizarre is AI's many regular-guy cheerleaders, pleased with the ability to issue commands to a machine and produce "art" to their specifications.

Over the past decade-plus, so many kinds of creative output have been flattened into a single word: *content*. Maybe this is the right word for what influencers do, filling a container—the platform—with the kind of material it was made to hold: square photographs, one-hundred-forty-character texts, six-second videos. But *content* is a disturbing word for art, as though a story or painting is merely filler inside a more important vessel. Efforts to remove the human from the art misunderstand what we look to art for.

AI art, at least so far, is remix. It sources from existing work that has been fed to it, creates according to instructions that have been fed to it, and yields a product that mimics an existing, recognizable medium: photograph, painting, story, song, poem, short video. It is a completed assignment. Artists, too, can work to specifications for an assignment. But artists have pesky human needs like "food" and "a roof," needs that run on money. AI art is a manifestation of an authoritarian fantasy: an "artist" that can't say no, and works for free.

The thing about artists—and humans more generally—is that

we are invested in refusal, in swerving around the instructions. As 2020 judge Tracy O'Neill said of her year's *Best Debut* anthology: "The short fiction I love best knows how to declare with beauty, 'I prefer not to.' It takes the page as a space to refuse what tends to be, unzipping barriers." Real art is unpredictable, its human makers defiant. It's not a simple transaction, but an ethos of resistance, refusal, reframing, dodging.

The topics and themes running through the different stories in this collection overlap and tangle: What do we inherit? How can we live through an unknowable future? What do we owe other people and ourselves? What dangers lurk in keeping the peace, or keeping up appearances? Who benefits? Even with these intersecting concerns, every story is unique. Each holds the secret history of what its author refused while shaping it.

A story directly engaged with fears around—and feelings of complicity in—authoritarianism and self-obliteration is Clara Mundy's "Schism in a Soul So Tender," set in a town where burgeoning sexuality causes young women to split into two selves: a chaste, bedridden self, conserving energy to do as she is told, and a sexual self in hiding, deemed nonhuman. Everyone believes that only one woman is real, the other a defective copy. Authority figures demand a particular violence they believe maintains order—but order over whom, or what?

The narrator of Dailihana E. Alfonseca's "Spanish Soap Operas Killed My Mother" contrasts island life, "when our homes had no glass on the windows" and "the air smelled vibrant and green," with her new life in New York, with its white walls, gray sky, and empty alleys. The rules and structures here weigh on her; she misses a life where iguanas would tell her omens and stories of her ancestors. In this new country, separation from the land is a separation from oneself. Everything is bordered and constraining, like the television screen hypnotizing her mother into someone she no longer knows.

Patrick J. Zhou's "Tàidù" follows a young American citizen, Jia, on a trip through China, his ancestral homeland. When the story opens, he's annoyed by two white Americans on the tour bus and their loud conversation about what they believe they are owed: English. Later, when Jia might be the only person who can help them out of a bind, he pretends not to understand—a decision he regrets. But in the moment, affected by the Americans' recent entitlement, his refusal feels like a reminder that he's an independent human being, not just one more resource for their consumption.

Beyond a divide between natural and artificial worlds, compulsory behavior and autonomy, these stories poke at the impossibility of knowing another person completely. Humans are capable of weird dissonance and surprising, ugly secrets. Sometimes we're disturbed by what we find ourselves capable of. In Faire Holliday's "Standing Still," Seneca panics and abandons her boyfriend's nine-year-old son alone at the park after she overhears him call her "my mom," an identity she can't stomach. Sometimes we're disturbed by what the people closest to us are capable of. In three hundred words, Verity McKay's "Filth" paints a devastating portrait of a marriage, child loss, and neglect. Sometimes we're shocked when we discover what we always knew, deep down, about someone. In Annabelle Ulaka's "My Grandmother's Feline Soul," a family buries their grandmother four times, unable to grieve her because she repeatedly rises from the dead. Each resurrection coincides with losses for her children: the death of a cat, a miscarriage, a fire that burns down a fashion house. Victory believes her grandmother is fueling each return by purposefully sacrificing what each child loves the most.

In place of shocking revelations, sometimes there's a slow awakening to a chasm between us and the people we think we know. In Ren Arcamone's "Allen," Liz and her boyfriend Phil have a running joke that their imaginary roommate, Allen, is responsible for their unwashed dishes and dead houseplants. With repeated invocations, Allen's personality and form flesh out—he seems so vivid, so recognizable. He's a big enough distraction for Liz not to see all she doesn't know or can't acknowledge about Phil. In Mengyin Lin's "Magic, or Something Less Assuring," Ting and Si-Bo are on a kind of anti-honeymoon trip in Morocco during the legally required "cooling off period" before they can finalize their divorce. Though they hold out hope that the desert might "rain fairy dust upon them," they can no longer ignore how different they've become from the people who first fell in love with each other eleven years ago.

Following the thread of the value of dodging, swerving, and reframing, Stephenjohn Holgate's "Delroy and the Boys" is a reminder to keep the balance between earning a living and really living. Delroy thinks he's in for a low-key performance for tourists with his band, making some extra money after his factory job. Then he finds out that his friends have been a little too friendly with the hotel manager's wife. Sweating, worrying, and playing their hearts out, the group devises a plan to make a getaway with their cash while their final song ends. Delroy is moved by the pressure-strengthened camaraderie among his friends and the happiness he hears in the last strains of the ending song, "as if, despite the stress and foolishness, something beautiful happen tonight."

In Sonia Feldman's "Outgrowth," the rigid worlds of science and the post-grad job market yield to the strange and unpredictable. At an isolated facility for plant researchers, Nomi can mostly ignore the emotional aftermath of a recent trauma; she takes comfort in the rigidity, the lack of intimacy between her and the seven other scientists, all men. Despite personal protective gear and compartmentalized information, boundaries blur—resist, swerve—between the researchers and the plants under their study. The ineffable connection between the humans and plants offers an eerie hope for the unknown possibilities of the future.

Jo Saleska's "Acts of Creation" is plagued by the narrator's anxieties of how impending motherhood might pigeonhole her into a particular, narrow definition of *woman*. She looks to the women around her for clues about what her future might hold—at a multilevel marketing essential oils party where "each woman is just another reflection of one woman, the real woman," and at the ceramics studio where her unapologetic (possibly magic?) tablemate philosophizes that art "should not behave in expected ways" or else "how will it shake our perception of reality?" Through some surreal experiences with a stolen sculpture, she finds her balance between the practical demands of new motherhood and surrendering to curiosity, play, and the unknown.

Lisa Wartenberg Vélez's "What Is Ours" felt fitting as the closing story in the anthology, for its narrator's ultimate explosive refusal to keep the peace. Coerced by her family to downplay her uncle's horrific crimes, she is seemingly the only one disturbed by everyone's complicity: all they didn't notice or willingly overlooked about him in the past, and the way they spin his jail time now as a "blessing in disguise" that transformed him into a praying man. A blessing, even though a brutalized child is dead. It's all too much— family pressure, religious pressure, enforced politeness, silence. Nothing can undo what that man did, but to be told to behave as though he didn't do it—it's too much. The family passes a phone around the room, making nice with the uncle. When it's the narrator's turn, she blurts something that makes the room gape, then turns her back on everyone and leaves. A second loud refusal with a brick and a Range Rover bursts the silence in another way, "a constellation of rage, its shards glittering at my feet."

What do we look to stories for? We want a sparkling range of representations of what it means to be alive. We want a sense of connection to the human, drawing on their life experiences, behind those representations—the human who actively shaped them. Humans have told stories for thousands of years. Human stories are older than money, older than corporations, older than information technology, older than content. They are ancient but ever-evolving, and hopefully immortal. There are stories only you can tell, told in a way that only you can tell them. Please, please do.

Many thanks again to this year's judges, Venita Blackburn, Richard Chiem, and Dantiel W. Moniz, who put together a real banger of an anthology, full of defiant human stories. Thank you as ever to PEN America and the Robert Jensen Dau Foundation. Thank you to the journals in this year's anthology—*Apricity Magazine*, *CARVE*, *The Cincinnati Review*, *Driftwood Press*, *Epiphany*,

HEAT, Hypertext, Nimrod International Journal of Prose and Poetry, Peatsmoke Journal, Waxwing, and *West Trade Review*—and to all journals that support writers at all stages of our human and literary evolutions.

Summer Farah

Sarah Lyn Rogers

Series Editors

BEST
DEBUT
SHORT
STORIES
2023

Editor's Note

Jo Saleska's "Acts of Creation" is a delightfully tactile story. From the opening scene's chill of the icy bath and the narrator's baby's foot pressing "into the pink lines on my stomach" to clay and soil beneath fingers, this piece lives in the body. "We are always touching," the narrator says of her baby, a line that holds a mixture of delight and suffocation. Throughout, we see the main character grapple with different models of womanhood—the friend with her multilevel marketing wine parties where everyone seems to look alike, and the artsy tablemate at her sculpture classes who doesn't shave her armpits and lets the clay speak to her hands. With a thrilling twist of the surreal as a stolen sculpture comes to life, Saleska examines the way motherhood can write women into narrative grooves and how much agency and identity this woman can claim. The language is deft and fluid, the images crisp, and the ending the sort that lodges between the ribs.

Wendy Elizabeth Wallace, Editor
Peatsmoke Journal

Acts of Creation

Jo Saleska

DR. MANN ASSURES ME RESTLESSNESS IS COMMON.
Besides, I've found ways to cope: essential oils, art classes, et cetera. In the mornings, I take cold baths. When the dawn breaks through the window above our tub, the bathwater shines like a prism. I slide in, let the cold snatch my breath, watch the blood escape my fingertips. I wring out like a dishrag.

Later, my husband pours water into the coffeemaker and explains why cold baths are a bad idea. He talks about oxygen deprivation, uses the word "hypoxemia," though he is an accountant and not a doctor—which I point out.

"Have you asked Dr. Mann what he thinks?" my husband says. He opens the refrigerator, pulls out turkey, cheese, mayonnaise. Assembles a sandwich. I tell him Dr. Mann suggested I avoid Jacuzzis, not cold baths. My husband licks a glob of mayonnaise from his pinky finger and fills a thermos with coffee.

"Any extreme seems reckless, though, don't you think?" he says. Coffee drips down the side of the thermos and forms a ring on the counter.

A lot is reckless for American babies that is considered perfectly unreckless elsewhere in the world: Coffee, for one. Cheese. Sushi. Saunas. Turkey sandwiches. Mayonnaise. Epidurals. Formula. In Paris, expecting mothers drink wine, enjoy cappuccinos, smoke cigarettes. I say all this to my husband as he gathers his things for work. He shrugs and kisses me on the nose.

"Whatever you think is best for our baby," he says, sliding out the front door into the heat of the morning. "It's your body. But do at least ask Dr. Mann."

ONCE A WEEK, I drive an hour and a half from Riverside to Venice Beach for ceramics class. There are ceramics classes in Riverside, but when one lives in the desert, one finds excuses to smell the ocean. I like the flow of traffic—all of us purpose-driven along the same cracked freeway toward the coast.

The studio is tucked inside a strip mall off Washington Boulevard, a half mile from the beach. From the parking lot, I cannot see the ocean, but I can smell the salt and sunscreen, can see hordes of people on their way to the beach, ice cream melting down their fingers, seagulls skulking close behind.

My tablemate is painting her clay sculpture when I arrive.

"What do you think of tourists?" she asks.

I shrug, pour green paint into my plastic tray.

"It's like, if you love L.A. so much, find a way to move here like the rest of us, you know?" She dips her brush in her tray of paint. "And if you don't want to move here, like, can't you find a way to be happy wherever you're from?"

I suggest to her that maybe some tourists will move to L.A. Maybe they're just trying the place on first to see if it fits, to see if they actually like it before they uproot their lives. My tablemate sighs heavily, sweeps paint onto her sculpture in hard, decisive strokes.

"Exactly," she says, "fucking cowards."

My tablemate is unbearably cool—black tattoos up her inner arms, unshaved armpits, a headscarf woven with gold thread. The rest of us are painting coil pots we made last week, all of which are wonky versions of the instructor's example: narrow at the bottom and wide around the middle like beehives. But my tablemate's sculpture is an infant-sized human kneeling in prayer, its long head is slightly cocked, its eyes gaping hollows. At once grotesque and elegant. She is painting it cerulean blue.

"I don't think art should behave in expected ways," she says when she catches me looking. "Otherwise, it's like, how will it shake our perception of reality?"

The instructor makes his rounds. He is barefoot and wearing board shorts, his hair a heap of blond curls. He smiles at my coil pot, which I'm painting green to match the nursery. "Great color," he says and winks. To my tablemate's humanoid sculpture, he says, "Hella rad, girl."

My tablemate scratches her eyebrow with her middle finger as the instructor passes our table. The thick, plastic smell of paint wafts in my direction, and I vomit into the trash can beneath our table.

DR. MANN ASSURES me that nightmares, too, are common. I have dreamt of giving birth to a torrent of water, which fills the room and drowns me, and to a two-inch-long adult man, a Tom Thumb, who sits on my shoulder and demands that I bake him a hundred tiny pies and knit him a hundred tiny sweaters. I have dreamt of giving birth to a child with six mouths, all of which are insatiably hungry, and of one with beady eyes on the tip of each of its fingers, which watch me wherever I go. Tonight, I dream that

I give birth to my tablemate's cerulean statue. It cries blue paint, leaves blue handprints all over our upholstery. My husband is disappointed because he was so hoping for a boy.

When I wake, sunlight pulses through the blinds, sending fiery lines across the bed. I draw myself a bath and slide into the water, letting the cold push the air from the pit of my lungs.

"MY GOD, YOU'RE glowing," my friend sings when I arrive at her house for Ladies Night. She squeals and claps her hands together. My friend is forever overreacting. She and the other ladies are already drunk and laughing. They gather around my friend's couch with glasses of wine, nibble at hunks of cheese from heaping platters. My friend's essential oil products are set out on the coffee table, gleaming in the lamplight. A few of the women set down their glasses to lift bottles of oil to their noses or rub some into the backs of their hands. The air smells like coconut and sage. I take a seat on the couch next to a woman with dark hair and wine-red lips. She leans into me, her eyes glassy. She is holding a thumb-sized bottle of oil.

"I rubbed this on my belly every night when I was pregnant with mine," she says, "and I swear to god, not a single stretch mark."

I nod and place my hands on my stomach. Without a drink, I'm not sure what else to do with my hands. When the woman asks what I do, I tell her I used to write poetry but now I'm experimenting with sculpture. I tell her I'm working on a piece designed to shake people's perceptions of reality. The woman laughs.

"No, no," she says, raising her voice, "I asked, *when are you due?*"

My friend clinks a spoon against her wineglass to call us to attention. She giggles at herself in the most charming way, thanks us all for coming, and explains how the products on the coffee table in front of us saved her life. The ladies smile in unison.

"I used to live my life by default," says my friend, "but now I live my life by design."

As she talks, I am struck by how the ladies watch her, each of them copies of the other, like we're in a house of mirrors, and each woman is just another reflection of one woman, the real woman: my friend, who is standing at the center telling us how it feels to have found her purpose.

And when she is done, there is hardly anything left to say. The ladies drain their glasses and make jokes about their partners watching their children ("Better get back before someone dies!"). They gather their purses, place orders, hug my friend goodbye. I buy three bottles of the thumb-sized oil.

When I get home, my husband is snoring. I go into the bathroom and remove my shirt, turn to the side. The pamphlet from Dr. Mann's office says that the baby is the size of a cucumber. An odd fruit to compare to a human fetus—long, green, warty. The nose of a fairy-tale hag. I pour oil into my hands and smear it over my stomach in swift circles.

MY TABLEMATE IS absent the day the instructor removes our pots from the kiln. When he calls us forward to collect them, I take my tablemate's sculpture, tuck it under my arm when the instructor isn't looking. No one notices, so focused they are on their own glossed creations. The parking lot smells like dead fish and waffle cones. The air above the blacktop churns with heat. I think

I might throw up, but I breathe deep and swallow it down. I set my tablemate's sculpture in the passenger seat, watch its glazed flesh shimmer in the sun as I drive. Every once in a while, I talk to it—try to explain myself. Its head is slightly cocked in my direction as if listening.

When I get home, I cradle the sculpture like an infant from the car into the house and up the stairs—a sort of test. It's warm from the sun and fits perfectly inside the crook of my arm. When I reach the landing at the top of the stairs, I imagine dropping the sculpture over the side, just to see what would happen: Would it shatter into a thousand pieces or merely bounce and roll?

Instead, I carry it into the nursery, which I've painted Glacial Green. We do not know the baby's gender. My husband wants to keep it a surprise: "There are so few surprises in life," he says.

I have poured my soul into this room. Spent days testing out shades of green on every wall. Scoured a dozen antique shops for the exact right rocking chair. Bruised my thumb and forefinger hammering together the bookshelves. I move the sculpture all around the nursery. I set it on a windowsill and step back to see how it looks, move it to a shelf, and then to another windowsill. After a while, I place it back on the first windowsill where it looks best after all. Then I pull a volume of fairy tales from the shelf and sit back in the rocking chair. There are many ways storytellers erase mothers: death by shipwreck, death by poison, death by plague, death by mysterious ailment, death by childbirth, death by fright, death by heartbreak, death by longing. Mother after mother buried in the ground beneath their children's journeying feet.

———

"IT'S REALLY GOOD, baby," my husband says when I bring him up to the nursery and show him the sculpture. "Maybe you should give up poetry altogether and focus on sculpting."

I slip on lingerie and make my husband sit in the kitchen and watch me cook stir-fry like I used to in the earliest days of our marriage. He loosens his tie, pulls me into his lap. We have sex on the couch in the living room. My husband's hands are damp, and his breath still smells like his morning coffee. He kisses my neck, presses his cold nose to my cheek.

"Is the baby okay?" he whispers.

When it's over, my husband kisses my belly, and then gets up to spoon the stir-fry into bowls. I lie and look down at my bare stomach. The skin along the bottom stretched and creased under the baby's weight. Spindly red lines crawl from my crotch to my belly button and along the tops of my thighs. My body is cracked desert earth, a road map with red-edged highways going nowhere.

The stir-fry is room temperature now and congealed at the top. Too salty. Yet my husband scoops dripping forkfuls into his mouth.

"Hey, did you decide to bring that down?" he says between bites. He gestures to something behind me. When I turn, there is the cerulean statue on the counter, its head cocked in our direction, eyes gaping. The statue is no longer positioned as if kneeling in prayer—instead, it is frozen in mid-stride, as if in a dead run to the edge of the countertop.

After dinner, I carry the sculpture back up to the nursery and place it in the proper windowsill.

———

THE DESERT SUN burns white-hot the day my first batch of product arrives. I wonder if it will ever rain again, or if all of California will shrivel to kindling and burn away. The product arrives in a white, glossy box and comes with a selling manual full of pictures of smiling women who all in one way or another resemble my friend.

"Who will you invite to your first Ladies Night?" my friend asks over the phone. I name a few mutual friends from college. "Those girls are already my clients," she says. "You'll need to branch out."

I picture myself as a tree—legs fused and immobile, roots reaching deep in search of water, my arms stretching toward the heavens, thickening, hardening. I tell my friend I'll work on it.

In the end, I invite a neighbor from across the street, an aunt, a cousin, and my mother-in-law. My friend comes, too, for "moral support." While my friend helps me arrange the product out on the kitchen table, my mother-in-law pours herself glass after glass of rosé and makes jokes about how she cannot wait for me to have the baby so that she can finally get revenge on my husband for all the sleep he deprived her of in her twenties.

"See these lines," she says, pointing to her forehead. "Your husband did this to me. I could have been an actress, you know, if it wasn't for the lines." The other women listen to my mother-in-law, laugh in all the right places. "Just imagine three years without sleep," she goes on. "It got so bad I started hallucinating piano concertos. I heard them everywhere—in my closet, in the shower, in the bottom drawer of the refrigerator."

I tell her she should have written down the music, tried to sell it for film scores or something.

"I never said the concertos were any good," she says, and the girls erupt.

My aunt chimes in, pointing to my cousin, "This one was so bad . . ."

From the corner of my eye, I see a flicker of movement outside the living room window. While the others talk, I slip out the sliding glass door and into the backyard. Moonlight pools across our heat-stricken lawn. A shadow paces back and forth against the back fence.

When I step closer, I can see that the pacing shadow is the cerulean sculpture. It takes a few steps, tiny feet crunching on dead grass, then raises a clay hand to the fence, feeling for something. As it moves, its glazed flesh glistens in the moonlight. It takes a few more steps, reaches the other clay hand to the fence. Like it's plotting an escape.

I hear the pop of the sliding glass door behind me and turn to find my friend.

"You should come back in and talk about the oil," she says.

I don't know what to tell the girls about the oil, so instead I pass it around, let them test it on the backs of their hands, soak it into their knuckles. My friend talks about the ingredients. She rubs the oil all over a saltine cracker and submerges the cracker in water.

"Watch how the cracker swells," she says. "The product lets moisture in but not out. Now imagine the cracker is your skin."

"Will it take care of the forehead lines?" my mother-in-law laughs. After a while, she buys a bottle and then wanders off to find my husband, who is hiding in his office. My aunt and cousin give me hugs, pat my stomach. My neighbor thanks me for the wine, says we should have done this sooner.

When they leave, I find the sculpture outside and carry it back into the nursery. I place it back in the proper windowsill, tell it to stay put.

IN THE EXAM room where I see Dr. Mann, a small print of the Virgin Mary and baby Jesus hangs. They wear flowing white garments, are suspended in a blue background that looks like a warped version of the night sky. The stable where Mary presumably gave birth is far in the background, warm and glowy. The scene is utterly peaceful. Shockingly clean.

I ask Dr. Mann if he's ever lost a patient before. He squirts gel on my stomach and presses in the fetal heart monitor. The sound of static fills the room.

"I may be losing my mind, but I make it a point to never lose patience," he says.

I don't know if I'm supposed to laugh.

"A little nervousness is common," he adds, pushing the monitor around in search of a heartbeat, and then: "The little one is hiding from us."

Dr. Mann makes this joke every time it takes more than a few seconds to find the heartbeat. I wonder how often he makes this joke to women in a single day. A month. A year.

"Ah, here we are," says Dr. Mann. The baby's heartbeat always frightens me with its loudness, like hurricane-force winds into the mouth of a microphone.

Dr. Mann says the baby is now the size of a jicama, so I pick a jicama up from the grocery store on my way home. I feel the shape of it in my hands, test the weight in my arms.

When I get home, my sculpture is missing from the nursery. I find it again in the backyard. It is kneeling in the dirt and digging a hole near the back fence with surprising efficiency. It scoops up mounds of dirt in its clay hands, tosses them over its glazed shoulder. Doesn't it know there is no way out? Beyond our yard is just another fenced-in yard. And then another. And another.

I scoop the sculpture up in my arms. Its clay flesh is hot to the touch and dusty from digging. It writhes. Pushes against me. I carry it upstairs, rinse it in the tub, and towel it off. I place it behind a locked glass cabinet in the dining room.

For dinner, I slice the jicama into strips and throw it in the stir-fry.

"It's different," my husband says, which, of course, is a polite way of saying he hates it.

When I fall asleep, I dream of a time when I was different. A time when I quoted the greats and sat on the beach at sunrise scrawling lines of verse into the sand. A time when I was a winged creature on the edge of a cliff. In the morning, I cup cold bathwater in my hands and drink. The baby kicks and kicks. I watch its little foot press into the pink lines on my stomach. We are always touching. I reach for a bottle of oil, read over the list of ingredients. I notice a note in small print: *Not recommended if you are pregnant or breastfeeding.* Motherfucker.

"HE STOLE MY sculpture," my tablemate whispers, nodding her head toward our instructor. "He denies it, of course." She is working and working her clay, rolling it out flat and then balling it back up, again and again. We are supposed to be making candlesticks.

When I ask her how she knows the instructor stole her sculpture, she shrugs. "A feeling," she says.

Outside the studio window, the marine layer hangs low and gray. A breeze carries a burger wrapper into a palm tree. I am more uncomfortable on my stool than I ever remember being. My ever-swelling stomach bumps up against the table, pain radiates down my lower back and thighs.

"I have this theory about misogyny," my tablemate says. "All of it, like *all* of it—the exclusion, the discrimination, the violence, the objectification—all of it stems from artistic envy." As my tablemate talks, she leans hard into her glob of clay, pressing and rolling, pressing and rolling. "God, it's not speaking to me today," she says, shaking her head.

My half-finished candlestick has begun to lean, so I smash it against the table, work it back into a ball.

"Anyway," my tablemate goes on, "I used to get, like, super bummed because all we ever hear about is men doing this and that—men writing all the books, making all the poetry, the art, the governments. And I'd always be like, but what have women made? And then it dawned on me. Women made all of humankind. We literally *make people*."

After class, I cannot bring myself to get back in my car. I walk up Washington Boulevard toward the ocean. The air is damp and cool. Cars rush by, press on their brakes, honk their horns. A rusty chain-link fence to my left blocks the sidewalk from the wetlands, which smell of sour decay. My hips ache, but it feels good to walk. When I reach the ocean, it's as gray as the sky above. I sit down in the sand, feel around for seashells. I find a charming blue rock, as blue as my cerulean sculpture. But when I look closely, it's just a piece of dried-out chewing gum.

I GIVE BIRTH to a baby girl. For twelve hours, she rips through me. My husband goes pale, vomits in a trash can at the edge of my bed. Dr. Mann pats him on the shoulder. Assures him that such a reaction is common.

The nurses set the baby on my chest—naked, wet, and writhing. I whisper to her: I made you. I made you. I made you.

They pack my underwear with layers of cotton, ice, and pads soaked in witch hazel, and they send us home. Outside our front door is another glossy package of product, along with my first commission check for sixty-six cents.

My husband takes our baby in his arms and starts the shower.

"I made it cold for you," he says.

I strip off my clothes, slide the bloodied underwear down over my knees and ankles. Blood drips from between my legs and blooms across our bathroom rug. I do not want to shower; I am afraid to get wet. I throw on my bathrobe and walk downstairs.

The door to the locked glass cabinet in the dining room is open, and the sculpture is gone. I push open the sliding glass door and step into the backyard. The backyard is empty, but there in the corner is the hole the sculpture dug—wide and deep. I walk over to it. Blood trickles down my thigh and calf and into the dry, golden grass. I kneel in front of the hole, which I realize now is a tunnel.

I climb inside.

The deeper I crawl, the cooler and softer the earth beneath my knees becomes. I dig my fingers into the soil, inch forward. Ahead, I see a light—an opening at the other end. A gentle, sweet breeze blows in through the opening, and I hear waves lapping against a shore. I see outlines of thick plants heavy with fruit. I am close now, can taste the salt of the sea.

And then, far behind me, I hear the tinny wail of my daughter. She is weeping, her body rattling, lungs sputtering. My breasts swell with milk.

I turn back toward the sound and begin the long climb out.

Jo Saleska lives and writes in St. Louis, Missouri. Her fiction appears in *Peatsmoke*, *Fauxmoir*, and *Bone Parade*. Her story "Insomnia," published by Alternating Current Press, was nominated for Best Microfiction 2023. She has an MA in literature from the University of Missouri, Columbia, and recently completed her MFA at the University of Missouri, St. Louis, where she was awarded the Mary Troy Prize for Fiction. Find her at josaleska.com.

Editor's Note

What initially struck me about Annabelle Ulaka's "My Grandmother's Feline Soul" was the strength of its characterization. Each sibling's personality expands under the pressure of grief until it clashes against the others'. The strangeness of a zombie grandmother almost takes a total back seat to the familial drama, which makes me laugh even as I mourn on their behalf.

The narrative makes literal what we all experience internally upon losing someone dear to us. As we come across the many places and things our loved one has left behind, including all those they never got to experience, memories resurface and we are forced to confront their death over and over until we are ready to let go. While the utter weirdness of an undead grandmother makes it easy for those who survive her to divert their minds temporarily from the pain of her actual passing, this repetition ultimately sets the stage for grief to finally take hold when the resurrections stop. It takes multiple deaths for Victory to process the loss of the most important person in her life, which feels deeply authentic. I find myself rooting for her as she tries to make sense of the bizarre goings-on and referee her siblings' petty arguments, all while trying to keep herself from crumbling. Victory's siblings—and Victory herself—are acerbic and blunt with one another but show compassion when it's truly needed. In other words, they're a family—one that actually functions pretty well, considering the circumstances.

There are many stories about grief, but "My Grandmother's Feline Soul" uses an unusual rendition of loss to reframe the experience, while at the same time never belittling its gravity. This story is a welcome and necessary addition to the ongoing literary discussion on losing a loved one, not least because it is fundamentally a celebration of what can make a person so hard to live without.

Gianni Washington, Associate Fiction Editor
West Trade Review

My Grandmother's Feline Soul

Annabelle Ulaka

THE EVENING BEFORE GRANDMA'S FOURTH FUNERAL, right when August showers swept the last sympathizers from our compound, I experienced my first panic attack. We were four in that living room. People often said madness and sanity were siblings in an endless tug-of-war. I never believed them. To me, a human's natural state is insanity. Maintaining levelheadedness is like swimming against a tsunami, emerging so worn out that we misinterpret unresponsiveness as sanity.

Madam Bianca, our closest neighbor, slammed our front door on her way out. She was an excessive mourner. Anyone who saw her rolling in dirt, screaming in that high-pitched voice, and cursing Grandma's nonexistent enemies would never have suspected she was present at Grandma's previous funerals. I released a long breath after watching her leave. These dramatic mourners always left me feeling emotionally clogged, like I'd not cried enough.

Minutes later, the living room became a graveyard. My younger brother, Junior, was counting our asbestos-filled ceiling tiles. He'd arrived hours ago in a charcoal-black Mercedes-Benz, kicked off his shoes, and ignored everyone's greetings.

On the other side of the room, Brother Thankgod was whistling. He flung his left leg over Grandma's chair, declaring his position as the newest authority. I almost laughed. If I'd been Grandma's first grandchild, I'd have sold my birthright.

Reaching for the TV's remote control, I tuned into a news channel. The headlines were so typical. *Inflation rate. Fuel subsidy. Workers on strike. Public holiday. Global warming. Elections.* People were queuing at petrol stations like normal human beings, while I and my siblings were burying our grandmother for the fourth time.

During the channel's third commercial break, the electricity went out. Someone began shuffling around in a bag. It had to be my sister, Endurance; she was the only one sitting in the dining area behind me. Click-clacks of her stilettos hitting tile echoed around the room. She transported Grandma's kerosene lantern from a side stool to the center table, pulling out a matchbox.

"Use my lighter, instead," Junior said.

Endurance scoffed. "A thief's lighter?"

If Grandma were alive, Endurance would never have voiced that thought. Junior was light-fingered, everyone knew. But Grandma banned the mentioning of it. When things disappeared, Grandma replaced them. After each expulsion, Grandma always found another school. When Junior absconded one morning with all of our jewelry, Grandma said jewelry was replaceable and her money was everyone's money.

"I don't need your stupid lamp, anyway," Junior said, pocketing his lighter.

Brother Thankgod hissed, "You need Jesus Christ."

When we were still kids in secondary school, Brother Thankgod became a church prostitute, renouncing our Roman Catholic faith, and forcing everyone to call him "Brother." He'd stormed into the living room one afternoon when Grandma was embroidering a cross onto her favorite skirt. Below Grandma's chair, Junior had sat like a devoted puppy. Brother Thankgod ran toward Grandma's seat, emptying a bucket of water onto Junior's head. He called it holy water. According to him, demonic possessions like kleptomania were exorcised, not condoned. I'd almost clawed Brother Thankgod's eyes out that afternoon.

"At least I have a job," Junior said, facing Brother Thankgod. "What do you have except Jesus Christ?"

Endurance laughed. "A job? You mean professional shoplifting?"

My brain was exploding. "Shut up, for God's sake! What is wrong with all of you? So Junior's now your problem? Grandma's a fucking zombie and none of you are talking about it. Take your nonsense outside this house. I'm not listening to any of it."

Brother Thankgod laughed. "Mummy's here to save you, Junior. Run to her; monsters are coming." He jumped up, feigning shock. "Look, Grandma's behind you. Run, run—"

Junior crashed into Brother Thankgod, sending them both to the floor. There was so much screaming, punching, slapping, and cursing. My stomach was on fire. I saw a full moon somewhere. What was that saying about a full moon after a storm? A king was born? A king was dead? Someone was screaming my name.

"You're tearing down the curtain, Victory," Voice A said. "Unclench your fists."

"The moon. The moooooon."

"I think she's gone mad," Voice B said. "Are you sure Grandma hasn't woken up again?"

Voice C hissed. "Do you believe that superstitious nonsense? Help me lift her up. She'll be fine in the morning."

I was probably in an ocean now, seeing as I felt weightless and wet. Barefooted people surrounded me. Grandma hated naked legs in her living room—she believed we'd catch pneumonia. Someone was crying; it sounded far away. The last thing I remembered was a voice saying, "Grandma, don't do this to us again."

TWO HUNDRED AND twenty-seven days ago, Grandma died for the first time.

I awoke that morning to Grandma's chickens crowing outside the house. Those chickens—like me—had somehow survived the Christmas festivities. Grandma's house stood atop a hill. It was the biggest mansion in our village, so secluded that it appeared haunted. Every December, Grandma turned the house into a museum. We'd have guests taking pictures in our bathrooms, picnicking on Grandma's carpet grasses, plucking fruits from our trees, and stealing our flowers.

One year, I caught a lady snoring in my bed. She'd slept on her back, knees bent, her shoes soiling my sheets. Pulling back the curtains, I'd closed my eyes and prayed sunrays would erase the figure in my bed. She didn't budge. I untucked the sheet from the bed frame, straightened her legs, wrapped her body like an Egyptian mummy, and rolled her off the edge. The fall almost fractured her right arm. Grandma pushed me onto a stool in our kitchen—the only private room in the house—after massaging the lady's arm. She accused me of having rich kids' syndrome. A baby once slept on her doorstep, she'd said, brown eyes, hungry stomach, like the lady in my bedroom. A little girl in a basket, with no owner. She'd given the child a home because no parent could lose a child up this hill. Nature had gifted her this infant, so Grandma gifted the child a home, naming her Victory. Sometimes, Grandma said, wiping my eyes, simple things like a stranger's bed meant the entire world to some people.

We discovered Grandma's lifeless body in her garden, arms and feet splayed out in the grass. Kneeling beside her, Brother Thankgod began checking for a pulse. Endurance held my forearm in a death grip. She must have sensed I was near collapsing. When Brother Thankgod stepped away from the corpse, he wouldn't look at me.

Her funeral was the talk of the town. Rumor had it that the governor was in attendance, overshadowing the presence of other traditional rulers. They shut down all major roads and hotels, slaughtered dozens of cows and chickens, and emptied bags of money on entertainers. I didn't recall any of this. The bottle of gin under Grandma's bed erased those memories.

What I remembered clearly was Brother Thankgod tapping me awake the next morning with news of Grandma's first resurrection. He told everyone that Grandma killed his cat. Milky had been healthy, according to him. When Grandma walked out of her grave, the cat collapsed.

Endurance called Brother Thankgod a dimwit, saying his cat chose death over putting up with him. They stood there arguing for hours. From the doorway, Junior beckoned to me. He pulled me up into a mango tree, where we sat watching Grandma trim a hedge of golden Duranta. She worked liked an ox. Her garden shears combed through the entire compound, scattering chopped flowers around the house like a mini cemetery. That scene reminded me of Auntie Jacinta, Grandma's only child. I pictured her under the sun, hands tight around the garden shears as she destroyed Grandma's flowers one afternoon. Junior had nicknamed her Crackie, though

Grandma hated that name. She believed her daughter was more than a common crackhead. But it was Grandma who disposed of Crackie at last when she grew tired of harboring an addict. She'd slapped the shears out of Auntie Jacinta's hands that afternoon, dragged her bags through the flower litter, and slammed our gate in her daughter's face. For months, Grandma watched that gate from our balcony, expecting Auntie Jacinta to emerge penniless, contrite, and pregnant with another Junior, Endurance, or Thankgod.

She never came back.

"Did we do something wrong, Victory?" Junior said, fisting a leaf. "Was it the grave? Should we have dug it deeper?"

"I don't know."

Junior sobbed. "I'm losing my mind here."

"Me too," I said, wiping my eyes. "Grandma spent a week in a freezer. A week! She's a fucking zombie and Brother Thankgod's talking about his cat?"

"What do we do now?" Junior said, cringing as Grandma waved at us.

"We wait," I replied. "And when the time is right, we add two more feet to Grandma's grave."

IN MID-APRIL, GRANDMA died for the second time.

I'd just stepped into my apartment a week after Easter Sunday when Gina, my flatmate, untangled herself from a painful yoga position. She was always exercising. Standing beside her, I looked like a polar bear facing its prey.

"Your grandmother is dead, Victory," Gina said, sweat pouring down her face.

My first thought was *Grandma is already dead.* Then I remembered everything I'd taught myself to forget. Those three months of emotional torture. After Grandma's first funeral, I never went back home. My nightmares became more frequent. I'd run to Gina's room at night, showing her Grandma's missed calls and text messages. She called it a passing phase, saying I was still in shock. Eventually, her diagnosis expired. Gina confiscated my mobile phone, added extra locks to her door, and posted my messages as sticky notes on the fridge.

"Call your sister," Gina said.

"Endurance?"

"Do you have another sister?"

There were days I refused to call Endurance my flesh and blood. As a kid, I'd find a toy frog in my closet, dead rats trapped under my pillow, a red wig in the shower, a skeleton on my bed. Grandma had a theory about pranks. She believed kids were naturally vile, and we'd grow out of that vileness someday. Endurance never grew up.

Gina threw my mobile phone at me. "Call her back."

"I can't."

"So what are you going to do?"

I began sobbing. "Don't you understand? I can't do this again, Gina. If Grandma wakes up, I'll lose my mind."

THE MORNING OF Grandma's fourth funeral, Brother Thankgod stood beside me, whistling a strange tune. I'd once begged him to teach me how to whistle. Having no musical skill was a social liability. Not only was I tone-deaf, but I also couldn't wiggle my waist without snapping a ligament. Brother Thankgod's reply

had been a throaty laugh. Talents were like human fingers, he'd
said; if it wasn't there, it wasn't there.

"I think it's going to rain," Brother Thankgod said. "Are you
sure you can attend the funeral?"

If only he knew how much I craved a storm. Whenever there
was a flood downtown, I'd watch people's belongings swimming
underneath us, thanking the heavens Grandma's house was on
a hill. Grandma nicknamed the mansion Our Little Planet. Up
here, she said, biology was just a thing of the mind—no one really
needed fathers, mothers, or grandfathers to complete their family trees, damn what the gossips said about us. The others never
agreed with this. Junior once asked Grandma, what kind of children just forgot about their mothers? I was familiar with this line
of questioning. Though Grandma had forbidden us from mentioning Auntie Jacinta's name around the house, Junior, Endurance,
and Brother Thankgod always found subtle ways to thwart that
rule. This time around, it made me angrier than usual. *Ungrateful
idiot*, I said to him. *Since you're so good at stealing people's things, why
don't you steal back your mother's love?* For weeks, no one talked to
me except Grandma. I learned to combat loneliness by memorizing
every crack on our roof, the amount of days it took carpet grass
to grow an inch taller, and the safest tree branches to sit on after
school. Ten years later, this place no longer felt like that refuge. I
fantasized about it sinking into the ground.

"I'm fine," I said to Brother Thankgod. "Stop worrying about me."

Endurance sighed behind me. "You should listen to him, Victory. You're still recovering."

One more mention of this nonsense and I might go crazy. "It

was just a panic attack, for goodness' sake. I'm not a fucking champagne glass. I'll survive."

"Why now?" Brother Thankgod asked. "You got drunk at the first funeral. You didn't attend the second funeral. You didn't even know there was a third funeral. Why are you suddenly interested in this one?"

I'd witnessed Grandma's third funeral on the internet, while searching for a music-streaming website. The headlines read: *Local woman resurrects again. Is Jesus Christ a lady? This woman has nine lives. Is she the cure for death?* Online, Grandma's house was almost unrecognizable. Reporters hung at every corner, some climbing our trees. They chased down Brother Thankgod, clawing at his kaftan, and begged for statements.

"Maybe Grandma's angry at me," I said, facing Brother Thankgod. "Maybe it's the reason she's coming back to life."

Junior appeared out of thin air. "I strongly disagree."

"Why?"

"You're the only one unaffected here, Victory. Think about it. Maybe your absence saved you."

"Stop!" Endurance screamed. "What's all this superstitious nonsense? Sometimes people die and wake up, for God's sake."

Brother Thankgod's glare burned a hole through Endurance's head. "Superstition? I lost my cat." His voice was shaky. "Didn't you see the autopsy report? She was healthy."

"It means nothing," Endurance said. "It was just a coincidence."

Considering how Endurance had almost lost it after Grandma's third resurrection, it surprised me that she was the least superstitious among us. I once believed in coincidences, too. Losing a pet was normal. Junior's wife's miscarriage synchronized with Grandma's second resurrection. That, too, was normal. The head-quarters of Endurance's fashion house burned down. Shit like that happened every day. But there was a limit to certain denials.

"This will be her last funeral," I said. "Grandma's not coming out of that grave today."

Endurance backed away from me. "Hell no. I'm not a murderer."

"Just shut up for once, Endurance," Brother Thankgod said, banging his head against the bars on the windows. "No one is forc-ing you to attend the funeral. If you're feeling fragile, stay home."

INDEED, IT RAINED at Grandma's funeral. There were no drums this time, no chickens, goats, or cows. Only three guests attended. They stood meters away from Grandma's grave like it was a black hole. Although we'd concealed Grandma's death from the public, I suddenly wished for flashing cameras. Rain always improved photography. I wanted everyone to see my dress, how it hugged my hips, how deep-necked it was, how my shoes made me taller than Earth. At least they'd have something else to talk about.

"Open the casket," I said to the pallbearers.

Junior grimaced. "Why?"

"What if she doesn't come back, Junior? I'll never see Grandma again."

Brother Thankgod glared at me. "Thirty seconds," he said.

The pallbearers dumped the casket on a wooden bench, flipping the cover. Grandma's skin was so pale. Even in death, she wore the cutest smile, though without her famous dimples. I adjusted the brooch on her left breast, parted her hair in the middle—the way she liked it—straightened a crease on her dress, and wiped a spot on her shoes. Morticians weren't always attentive to details. My eyes were leaking. *Shit!* Where was my hair dryer?

"What else do you want, Victory?" Brother Thankgod said, startling me. "Do you wish to count her teeth, too?"

I sniffed. "Grandma's dead."

"That's not new."

"You don't understand," I said. "She's not coming back."

WHEN THE LAST guest left our compound, Brother Thankgod knelt beside Grandma's grave, placing his right ear on the bump. The rain had reduced to a drizzle. Every drop sounded like Heaven receiving Grandma's soul.

"She's gone," Endurance said behind Brother Thankgod. "Even if you listen till tomorrow, she's not coming back."

Brother Thankgod ignored Endurance, turning to face me. "What did you do, Victory? Grandma couldn't have spared you. She stole something from everyone here. What did she steal from you?"

I thought about Grandma's first rule, the one she'd always barked at us: *If it doesn't have teeth, it's harmless.* "Maybe Endurance is right," I said. "People die and wake up sometimes."

Junior hissed. "Spare me that nonsense. Have you witnessed a cat being killed before? They don't just collapse. They fight for their lives."

Brother Thankgod sobbed. "Tell them. My Milky was strong."

"You had your cat, Brother Thankgod," I said. "We all know

you loved her. Everyone here had something Grandma could steal. What do I have?"

"Me," Junior said. "You have me, Victory."

"Then why aren't you dead?"

Endurance kicked a twig. "Because you loved Grandma more than him. Think about it. If she truly stole things from us, wouldn't she have taken the best?"

The best? Who could determine what people loved best? Endurance walked through fire to establish her fashion house, Brother Thankgod would sell his soul for Milky's, and Junior almost bankrupted his company trying for a child. But these things deserved love. Just like the taste of midnight coffee, the smell of first rains, the euphoria of drunkenness, and the color of flowers. Was it possible to cherish one above the other? Grandma always preached about true love, how we'd find it only once in life. *Worship it,* she'd say, *because something else will take it from you, eventually.* Whenever she made that statement, I'd think about Auntie Jacinta. She was the reason Grandma could not love us enough.

Suddenly, everything made sense. How much Grandma hated Brother Thankgod's cat. How she always found faults in Junior's fiancées. Why she'd refused loaning Endurance capital for her fashion house. How much she hated herself. Mostly, how much she hated love. And love was everywhere—so difficult to steal the right one. Grandma knew this. For this reason, she never called Junior a thief. Thieves were not lazy. They watched, learned, and attacked. They stole that which no one could replace. They left you feeling empty.

My head was swimming. I stumbled into Junior, gripping him for support and crying into his shirt. A hand patted my back while the other guided me toward Grandma's grave. Kneeling beside it, I placed my right ear on the bump, just the way Brother Thankgod had earlier. Endurance imitated me, kneeling at the other side. Junior was next. Brother Thankgod last.

"Did you hear anything?" Endurance asked Brother Thankgod afterward, seeing as he was closest to her.

"No."

"What about you, Junior?"

"No."

"Victory?"

"Birds were singing," I said.

Junior laughed.

"You're all deaf," Endurance said, fighting a smile. "Did you really not hear anything?"

"We don't have all day, Endurance." Brother Thankgod dusted his knees. "What did you hear?"

She smiled. "Birds were singing."

Annabelle Ulaka is an emerging writer who believes in the magical bond of family and often sources this family connection as her major inspiration. She lives in a little town in the north of Nigeria, where she raises three black cats nicknamed Little Tigers. Her greatest aspirations are writing an international bestseller, learning to dance, and visiting one-fourth of the earth's countries.

The first thing we noticed about Stephenjohn Holgate's "Delroy and the Boys" is that old Proteus of fiction: voice. It's so hard a thing to define, and much harder to find, but voice is, I have found more and more, quite often the propellent for the very best prose. The strongest stories carry their readers along even when they're not sure, at the outset or at the conclusion, quite where they're going. For as much else as it achieves, "Delroy and the Boys" is an exceptional example of that idea—not only in its use of patois and idiom (although that was immediately compelling to many of us, and A Confederacy of Dunces was brought up more than once in our internal discussions) but in voice as a tool toward narrative intention. Voice, for as slippery and enigmatic as it can be, is really about intentionality. Especially in the first person, as in Holgate's story, but in all writing, how one describes something colors and shapes the manner in which it is presented to the audience. Voice is, at its core, diction, which is word choice, and word choice is what gives a story its intent. When we, both at West Trade and generally as literary citizens, bemoan writing (our own or otherwise) that lacks direction—that seems in some way to not hunt down and devour the beast it means to chase—we're sensing that lack of narrative intention, that lack of voice. The best writing immediately and unabashedly pursues its goal and leaves the reader with a sense of the importance of its subject matter, of how it was presented, and of the significance of those things as a gift to carry with us. "Delroy and the Boys," primarily via its exceptional voice, achieved those aims and left a relatively easy decision for the fortunate *West Trade Review* editorial staff.

D. W. White, Fiction Editor
West Trade Review

Delroy and the Boys

Stephenjohn Holgate

BOY, I LAUGH SO TIL. WAS SUPPOSED TO JUST BE A little show up at the hotel, nothing too too serious. Cultural thing. Me, Bongo Barry, Tony, and Earl. Wasn't any problem for me, my work down at the factory finish four o'clock sharp and that give me enough time to go home, iron shirt and pants, and pick up my guitar. Bongo don't care either because him just going to ride up the hill to the hotel with him old motorbike him use to go beach and sell him merchandise, rumba box tie up on the back. Earl? Earl dependable as long as you say the word rum. But Tony, Tony always in some kind of trouble, usually with a married woman or two. So, the first thing is to find him.

I finish at the factory and cycle down to the house, set meself up, and gone again to Tony house. I figure it worth a shot, sometimes him surprise me and worse come to the very worst we put Earl on banjo and don't use no maracas tonight. The hotel boss is a man named Utchinson and him rather you turn up and do a bad show than no show. Him also pay quick and give regular work and in these hard times you can't overlook that. Him also have a piece of wife there. Father God, pure headache. Morning, noon, and twice a nighttime. Headache. Rumor was having it that Tony did have thing with her one time, but she make it out of board house and into big house. And although she reach up she keep looking down and no man with black skin safe. Some people only looking away and never looking around.

When I reach out by Tony his mother sitting on the verandah singing Give Me Oil in My Lamp really sweet. I surprised that bird and beast not congregating round like in one of them cartoon movie because is the nicest sound I hear all day. I don't know why Tony sound like S90 engine that going to conk out anytime soon. I mean he in tune, but it is not a smooth sound that this man produce. After I listen for a while I say, Miss Joy, Tony about?

That worthless, good for nothing johncrow? That disappointment? Him up at the hotel. Or at least that him tell me. That boy bring more crosses into me life than I think I can bear. And him never think about him mother yet. When I dead is then him going to start worry about me and then it too late. Too late.

I know she ready to carry on with full force, so I make my excuses and tell her that I meeting Tony up at the hotel. When Miss Joy realize that Tony telling the truth she look even more upset, like she was getting ready for a real fight and now she going to have to find something to vex with him about. I don't stay to find out and I tear up the hill so we can have a quick tune up and practice before we out in front of the tourists. Just because them don't know the difference between calypso and mento don't mean they don't deserve the real thing.

The hotel, if you never see it yet, is one of those old estate-style house with a few cottages dotted about the place. You wouldn't believe this bit was never a plantation, unless you realize say it a little bit too close to the sea and there's not that much good farmland around it. These people not try to get nothing too real all the same, them looking for a little escape. Them escaping here and a

whole bunch of Jamaicans looking to escape there. On the private
road leading up to the hotel they have a little hut with a lonely
guard that sit there. If you come late at night the guy there usually
catching a quick sleep but as is early him looking wide awake and
bored. One look at me in bright print shirt and him know that we
a part of the cultural show tonight: what passing for kumina danc-
ing, a little fashion show, some idiot doing limbo and mashing up
his joints and us playing little music. Once in a while they have a
little reggae thing as well and Bongo usually try to get pay twice
by playing rumba box for us and then drums for whoever playing
after. That don't usually work and more time him only get a pay for
the night.

When I reach round to the ballroom where everything taking
place I see Tony and Earl lean up against one of the pillars looking into the main area and Tony smiling big big. So I lean up my
bicycle by the coconut tree and go over to them. When I look in is
a troupe of dancers doing something that I think is supposed to be
kumina. Black, gold, and green costumes, woman with their hair
tie up and hands holding up their skirt. But they look bored. Really
bored. And I can see why. The musician them just going through
the paces, no liveliness on the drums at all at all. Like the drums
themselves drink a white rum and done for the night. When I
look over on the musicians I see Bongo there betwixt everybody,
looking foolish. Him trying the double pay thing and it might even
work if Utchinson feel in a good mood.

As I look at Bongo I notice sweat peeling down his forehead. I
mean, the man look like him just come out of a river: head, nose,
chin, even the shirt look like him been walking through deep

water. And him eyes bouncing up and down and looking every damn way. I hope him don't smoke too much ganja before tonight because I can't have us sounding like this mausoleum music, this dead house disco. No Boss.

Now this time I hear Earl with one piece of belly laugh and Tony looking gray. Tony scratching him head like him have chigger and bouncing up and down. Well, with Tony is always something, so I don't even bother myself because we have to sort out what songs we doing. So we peel down behind the gazebo they have on the other side of the lawn to at least tune up and make some decisions. Whatever going on with Bongo, him know all the songs and is probably the best musician so I don't have any worry about him being able to fit in. We start up with a few of the classics, you know, Iron Bar, Rookumbine, and Solas Market. In the end we make a decision that, really, is slackness and liveliness that the tourist them want so we plan to do Big Bamboo, Talking Parrot, Day-O (because for some reason is the onliest one that the tourist them seem to know), and finish with Shaving Cream.

While we working through Rookumbine this white man sidle up next to Tony, nodding him head and bouncing up and down like him have some kind of foot problem.

You fellas sound alright. I mean I really like your whole vibe, the whole island thing. You want a cigarette? I really, really like the sound and all, y'know, reminds me of my honeymoon, my wife passed on a couple of years ago, y'know, but we stayed at a little place out in Ocho Rios and they had a group that sang that song and we just loved it, y'know, and you fellas sound so good, I just wondered if you know any Jim Reeves? My Celia used to love Jim

Reeves and these guys in Ocho Rios played a couple of Jim Reeves songs and we danced to them, I'd really appreciate it if you fellas could play one of his songs, I mean if you know any, y'know.

This man clearly under more than two, but he friendly nuh backside and handing out cigarettes like candy. Even One-Foot Trevor pass by and get one. Well, me and the boys only know He'll Have to Go. Personally, I prefer Conway Twitty and Hank Williams, but that's another matter. Well, when we say we going to play a Jim Reeves the man start bawl and shake hand and handing out more cigarette and putting money in everybody hand. One-Foot Trevor pass by again and get a five hundred dollar even though he don't have no music in him soul.

Next thing Bongo run over to us and start with how him need to leave and go home and how them going to murder him. Well, we done take this white man money and just because Utchinson pay him don't mean the rest of us can go back home with only we two long hand. So I give it to him and call him every name I know from ginnal to johncrow. And still Bongo sweating. Heavy sweat like raindrops dropping off the end of his nose.

Look star, is Hutchinson. Him not going to pay me. I lucky if I escape with all of my bone intact. Jah know, star. Look, is me and Claudette, Miss Hutchinson, I was dealing with the thing and then she find out that I was also dealing with her sister, Marcia, so she take it upon herself to talk with Marcia and who should she catch with Marcia but Hutchinson so then she go say is alright because she done give him bun with me and Tony, so now him ready to deal with the two of we.

Earl just skinning teeth the whole time. Now the whole of we

in one quandary. Me and Tony need the money. Plus, we done get
paid for the Jim Reeves song so we have to go on.

Finally Earl finish the drink of rum him been holding the entire time and say, I go handle this, but all a unnu owe me. And,
laughing like a jackass, him wander off towards the main reception.

Now, Bongo still looking nervous and Tony smiling, but smiling like is not really any kind of happiness him feeling. I make
them finish the warm up and we go and wait for the fashion show
to done. I can't even enjoy the girls them in their dresses because of
these two fool-fool friends of mine, so I look over at the table that
Utchinson sitting at and I glad is not me him vex with.

Utchinson is a big, big man, and he used to do little wrestling
or something when he was at school in America. Not that foolish
wrestling that you see on the TV. The one that look like you could
really murder a man with. Sure, him have that sort of softness
that come from being one of those high-color business-running
Jamaicans that never have to worry about whether light or water
going to get lock off, but that is just a soft layer over a hard object.
Rumor was having it that one of the reasons him come by the hotel
was that him did go sailing with the business partner and when
him come back is just him one and the boat. I don't know, but is so
the story go. Utchinson sitting there looking like he want to bruck
something up and next to him Claudette pursing up her lips and
smoking a cigarette and looking like she having a great time. Clapping loud loud when the models walk by and completely ignoring
the time bomb she sitting next to.

Earl come back and push money in everybody pocket. Was
Vivette controlling the payment tonight and she owe me a favor so

we get cash up front. When show done I not staying around for no after-party and entertainment. Straight home. My domino partner Derrick have space in his car for me and I leaving straight afterwards.

Delroy, you have your bicycle?

I nod.

Well keep it close by. Unnu two have to find a way out, me do more than enough for you. And with that Earl smiling again like what about to happen is no problem.

Oh, by the way, we have to do that Jim Reeves song. You know the one where him call up the woman and tell her she must left her man. Yes boy, glad me name Earl and not Tony or Barry. And with this Earl popping big laugh and rubbing him head.

Well now, when the fashion show done and it come to the other cultural part of the evening we take up our position in the middle of the room: Bongo have the rumba box and sitting on it, me with the guitar softly in my hands, Tony with banjo squeeze up in him hands, and Earl smiling under him felt hat with the two yellow maracas in him hands.

Good evening ladies and genkle men, Earl start with him sweet tourist voice, we are here to give you a little mento. Mento is the ancestor of reggae. Some people don't know that it's different to calypso, but that's alright, we going to give you the realness now. One, two, three.

And so we start with Day-O, because that have a nice feel and the tourist them will feel safe singing about banana and rum drinking. Tony looking a little nervous on the banjo, but he covering it well and it don't seem to seize up him hands. Bongo still sweating like hell and I worried we going to wash away with the amount of perspiration falling off his head.

Then I take a peep at Utchinson. Backside. The man look like him ready to murder everybody in the place. Claudette next to him smiling and clapping as we launch into Big Bamboo and I start to wonder if we really make the right choice with the songs or if we making things worse in the long run. People in the audience laughing along to how the big bamboo stand up straight and tall and how it pleases one and all but Utchinson not looking too pleased. Utchinson look like when you pass one of them bad dog and them wonder whether or not to rush you and bite up you foot. Or how bull look before them charge. So now I get really frighten because I can't afford to be no innocent bystander in whatever going to happen. I start to look at my bicycle by the coconut tree.

Alright, who singing the Jim Reeves song? Earl ask. I know for damn sure I am not singing anything like that. I'm just looking at my bicycle and thinking about how quick I can ride home. Coward man keep safe bone and I like my bone them.

Me can sing that one, Bongo say. And I really start to wonder about the state of this man brains. Bad enough that him turn Joe Grind with Utchinson wife, but now him going to sing about it? I was just about to raise my objections when Bongo start sing about sweet lips and phone. Him hands slapping the rumba box and Tony join in prompt on the banjo. Well, now I don't have no choice but to strum the guitar and keep the rhythm going. I take another peep over to the boss table and see him changing color. Two minutes ago him was just another brown man, now I swear the man turn devil red. Claudette stop smile now, which even worse because she looking at Bongo like the man is only singing to her. And the truth is Bongo sound like a real crooner. But that not helping the situation. If them catch you with a next man woman you can't stand up in front of everybody and sing about how him have to go. I start sweat now, so if you look up on stage is only one person keeping them cool. Earl smiling and shaking maracas and working the crowd still. Everybody else look serious or sweating and I wonder how the hell we going to get out of here without problems. I know what Utchinson is like. Him is a man that look at what him do and judge whether it was the right decision long after everything mash up and done.

Alright, Earl whisper to us, we do the Talking Parrot and straight into Shaving Cream. When we singing as we come to the last verse I want you to stop playing, Bongo, and take the rumba box out that way. Him point towards the opposite side of the concourse. Tony, you go out the same way but keep playing. Before the last chorus you can stop playing as well, Delroy. Go to your bicycle and take off down the hill. I going to get these tourists to sing along with me and the maracas and I going over to Hutchinson to talk to him about some things. That should cover enough time for all the rest of unnu. He don't have no problem with me and everybody done get pay. All of you owe me a rum.

I don't owe nobody a raas. But before I can raise my objections them take off with the talking parrot song, Earl singing sweet sweet about how him nearly lose him life in Spanish Town because a talking parrot reveal him relationship with a married woman. I mean we really should have changed up the playlist when the problems make themself known. My eyes catch the American we talk to earlier and he smiling and crying and giving me thumbs-up, so at least one person leaving tonight in a good place. Next thing I know Earl singing Shaving Cream and I know I have to pay attention and can't just let my fingers follow while my mind is in other places. The crowd really getting into it and them laughing and clapping. Them wouldn't believe that this not a real traditional song and is actually American. From they hear the Jamaican accent them don't know which way is up and what come as truth. Some people easily distracted like that.

Before I realize, Bongo and Tony peel off and trying to walk like is part of the performance. Only the trail of sweat from Bongo big head is a giveaway. Earl reaching the end of the song and I start tiptoeing my way to the bicycle. I moving slow. I want to move a little faster. But I take my time and swing the guitar across my back and get ready to take off. I hear Earl and the whole crowd singing Shaving Cream. I can hear the happiness them feeling and for a second I feel really good. As if, despite the stress and foolishness, something beautiful happen tonight and before the feeling can go I jump on the bicycle seat and scatter down the hillside.

Stephenjohn Holgate was born in Port Antonio, Jamaica, and is currently packing up his life to move to Aotearoa/New Zealand. He read English at Oxford University and has an MA in classical acting from the Central School of Speech and Drama. A member of the Writing West Midlands Room 204 writer development program, he was one of the Bridport Prize's inaugural Black Writers in Residence in 2022.

Editor's Note

"Allen" is the perfect example of the kind of fiction we're always looking to publish in *HEAT*: a story full of quick-witted, clever observations that may seem fleeting at first but hold a secret power to linger in the mind of the reader. That this is Ren Arcamone's first published story is, in a way, wonderfully beside the point—with "Allen," she arrived fully formed in our pages, immediately at home among a mix of writers of poetry and prose from Australia and around the world.

Alexandra Christie, Editor
HEAT

Allen

Ren Arcamone

PHIL AND I HAVE A MAKE-BELIEVE HOUSEMATE—WE call him Allen. Allen is a real jerk. Allen never cleans the bathroom, leaves the fan on when no one's home, and only half empties the dishwasher. Allen lets the laundry stay out on the line for so long that all our jeans are sun-faded, and he alone is responsible for the murder of our beloved houseplant, Fernie Sanders. He never vacuums. He never takes the dog for a walk. "Fucking Allen," we say, when we wake up with hangovers and the kitchen counter is splotched yellow with turmeric stains. "Fucking typical." Allen hides Phil's shaving cream the morning before his job interview at The Orchard, a boutique advertising agency. "Allen!" Phil yells at the bathroom mirror. "Allen, you bastard! Get your own bloody shaving cream!" In the end he uses mine and he leaves the house smelling of coconut, but he gets the job. On the weekend we go out for cocktails and enumerate Allen's flaws.

"Allen's from Vaucluse and he grew up with a maid. That's why he doesn't know how to do the ironing."

"Allen went to an all-boys college and misses the days he used to shave off people's eyebrows."

"Hmm," I say. "I think Allen's more sensitive than that. Allen did hazing in college, but now he says he's reformed. He's a Sensitive New Age Guy. But he's still afraid of women's periods."

"Right. He's scared of female bosses and bisexual men."

"Jesus. Grow up, Allen."

"Allen tells people he read *The Game* 'ironically.'"

"Allen's Tinder profile is a quote from David Foster Wallace."

"I bet he hasn't even made the bed. Fucking Allen."

And sure enough, when we get home, gin-drunk and already regretting our Saturday brunch commitment, the bedsheets are tangled and the pillows are slumped in distant corners of the room, like victims from a bomb blast. Our dog, Archimedes, is huddled under the sheet clump and seems surprised to see us.

"Meedy!" Phil says. "You know better! Off, come on, off!"

"Actually," I say, coming back to the bedroom with two glasses of water. "I actually think it is your turn to do the dishes. Will you do them tomorrow?"

"For you, Liz? Anything." He grabs me and kisses me and water sloshes onto the floor and a little bit onto the dog. I put the glasses on the bedside and fumble with his zipper and we roll into bed, struggling out of our clothes. I bite his neck and he yelps.

"Be quiet," I say in his ear. "You'll wake Allen."

In the morning we lay in bed and groan for an hour. "Get me a Berocca," I say.

"Get it yourself," says Phil. "Can I have some water? Where's that glass?"

"Where's *my* water?" I say. "You stole them both!"

The two glasses are still filled up and sitting in the sink.

"You must have been sleepwalk-cleaning," I say, although the rest of the house shows no evidence of this.

"Creepy move, Allen!" Phil says to the ceiling.

This is the day the spoons go missing. We don't notice it, at first. We drink Bloody Marys at brunch with Phil's theater friends, and when we get home Phil takes a three-hour nap and I lie on the couch with Archimedes for TV1's Nineties Nostalgia Fest, catching half of *She's All That* and the entirety of *The Truth About Cats & Dogs*. I get up to make myself some green tea with honey. There are no spoons, not in the dishwasher or the dish rack, none hidden under the risotto-encrusted pan soaking in the sink. I stack the dishwasher, slowly. No teaspoons, dessert spoons, soup spoons, zero.

"Phil!" I yell. "Do we *own* spoons?"

We are adults, I mean legally. We've been out of university for a year and both of us have landed full-time jobs: he in digital, me in copywriting, which is another way of saying we both work in advertising. We have money and independence and a chore roster marked out on a whiteboard that we both routinely ignore. And we throw dinner parties. We definitely own, or owned, at least for some period of time, multiple spoons.

"I'm asleep!" Phil shouts back.

We carry on with life, sans spoons. I keep meaning to go to Big W and forgetting about it, and then Phil starts stealing cutlery incrementally from the kitchen at his work, and we decide we don't actually need more than four spoons, total.

Friday night drinks at The Tipple are now a regular fixture. It's exciting to have real jobs to complain about and enough money to drink pinot gris past happy hour. We get there before the rush and secure two swivel seats at the front window so we can stare out onto the footpath at all the people with silk blouses and mortgages and opinions about the economy. "Do you think we could pass for them?" Phil says dreamily.

"Someday."

He clinks his glass to mine. "Allen," he says, "is a wine snob."

"Allen thinks Japanese whiskeys are overrated. But only because he read it in a men's magazine."

We reflect. My pencil skirt is slippery on the barstool and the sky is doing that red-gold Sydney sunset. I feel like I'm melting, but slowly and pleasantly. Phil takes a noisy wine gulp.

"Allen self-describes as 'an audiophile.'"

"Yes," I say. "And he has the complete discography of The National memorized."

"Wait!" says Phil, laughing. "What's wrong with The National?"

"*You* know," I say. "*You* know. That The National sounds like, umm, a Catholic schoolboy discovering atheism? Like . . . pretending not to cry during Robin Williams's speech in *Good Will Hunting*?"

"I liked *Good Will Hunting*!"

"But you know what I mean? How The National sounds like awareness-raising for the stats on male suicide?" I pause. "Too far?"

"No, I hear it." Phil swirls his wine, all moody resignation. "The National sounds like a Polaroid of your pilgrimage to Hemingway's cabin."

This is why I love Phil.

"But I do still like The National."

"That's okay," I tell him. "You're bisexual. It's not the same."

October is ending. We want to throw a party that is sort of a Halloween party but is mostly a party for no reason, and so we hose down the plastic lawn chairs and make rice-paper rolls and buy two boxes of Banrock wine: goon, but fancy goon. Phil and I go as Thelma and Louise, but our friends assume we're cowboys.

Everyone turns up late, dumping their bags on the bed in the spare room. Archimedes is chill but he begs for party pies and then throws up in a potted peace lily.

"Can't wait till Allen moves out," Phil says dramatically.

"Who's Allen?" say four people.

We explain. Allen's kind of a slimeball. He describes himself as "a gentleman." He thinks all his exes are psycho.

"But is he good in bed?" asks Jolene, who is dressed as Ginger Spice.

"He's afraid of cunnilingus. But his family is rich. He has an excellent credit score."

"Does he have a type?"

"Girls who wear feathered headdresses to music festivals."

"I think he's my boss," says Richelle, who "works in sales" for Billabong, which I recently realized is different from working in retail. "Does he talk about business getting 'actualized'? But he also talks about the time he got 'enlightened' on ayahuasca?"

Phil finds this very funny. "Actually," he says, "in that case, I work with a floor full of Allens."

"Jesus," says Jolene. "Keep me on the dole." But later in the night she says she got offered a bit part on *Neighbours*, so it's hard to feel sorry for her.

In the morning there's a scattering of bodies on the sofas, the spare bed. I collect glasses and dead bottles in a fugue state while Jolene makes coffee. We discover the dishwasher is broken and do the cups by hand. Phil emerges at noon, looking like his eyes have been sewn shut.

"I forgot to tell you," I say. "Allen told me you were going to vacuum the floors tomorrow. On account of how my parents are coming to stay next weekend and on account of how I did them last month."

There's a fraction of a second where Phil's face gets all closed-off and contrarian. But he catches himself. "I wish I knew when Allen was going to reach adulthood, you know?"

In the afternoon, when everyone is gone, we smoke the rest of a joint that Jolene left on the windowsill, which softens the hangover and has the effect of making our clean apartment seem miraculous and beautiful. I take a shower and Phil sits in the empty bath to keep me company, but my brain fogs over and I can't keep the thread of our conversation, and when I tune back in Phil is singing a made-up song.

"I need to be different," I tell Phil, tearful, as he folds me into bed.

"What?" he says. He touches my forehead, like I'm feverish. "What do you need?"

All I know is there's a terrible wrongness sitting on my chest, mute and heavy like a stubborn cat. This happens sometimes. When I was in high school I would feel it the night before exams, as though the test had already happened and I was sitting with the uncorrectable idiocy of my mistakes, and nothing, not even doing the test, would set things right. It feels like having a spyglass that looks directly into the moment of my death, and the me that is still me is trapped in a terrible puckered face with bad-smelling dentures and I know I have frittered away my entire life. But I can't say that. Instead I say, "My hair is still wet." Phil doesn't catch this.

"Other people need to be different," he says. "Not us."

A week goes by. Mondays are awful in the world of adult jobs,

but so are Tuesdays, and also the other days. We drink wine and
watch Netflix when we eat dinner, and we try not to annoy each
other about the dishes, and somehow things stay clean enough.
But on Thursday Archimedes goes missing. I am inconsolable. We
stand on the road in the early evening and yell down street alleys.

"Meedy! Sir Archimedes Snufflepaw! Come home and we'll
feed you peanut butter every day! Meedy!"

Phil walks me home with his arm around me. I chew a hang-
nail with Terminator focus.

"He'll turn up," says Phil. "He's a collie. They're the cleverest
kind."

"And the bravest," I say.

"Yeah. Meedy's real brave and smart. I bet he had to go save
someone, you know? Or solve a crime. He's way more competent
than we are. He's probably busting up a drug-smuggling ring as
we speak."

My parents turn up with their suitcases that evening. My
mother strokes my hair while I lie on the sofa.

"Did you leave the back gate open?" she asks, both sympathet-
ically and unhelpfully.

Phil walks into the room holding a teapot. The carpet is very
clean. "We're blaming Allen," he says.

"Who's Allen?" says Dad.

"Our dropkick housemate," says Phil, glancing at me. I shoot
him my dagger-eyes. I don't want to play Allen. I just want my dog
back.

"Here," says Mum. "I'll rustle up some food for us. We'll call
the shelter in the morning."

But Archimedes is not at the shelter. Phil draws up a

classy-looking MISSING poster in Illustrator and prints off a ream at work the next day, and in the evening my mother and I wander round the neighborhood, stapling Meedy's sweet face to telegraph poles. Mum pats me periodically, like I'm the dog. I aim for a brisk, no-nonsense smile, but my eyes keep watering.

"He'll turn up," says Mum. She gives me a long look. "You know there's always a space for you back home, don't you, if things don't work out here?"

"I thought you liked Phil!" I say.

"We do, we do. We just . . ." She trails off, staring up at a pair of sneakers strung over a power line. "We worry sometimes."

"We're doing fine for ourselves," I say. She frowns at my tone. "My job's fine. Phil's job is very stable and the management is actually very chill. He's really committed. Last week we bought a Nutribullet."

"Sometimes kids move out of home for a few years," she says, carefully. "And then, for whatever reasons, they need to move back for a period of time. And that's okay. I just want you to know you're always welcome back home."

I punch the stapler to a telegraph pole with both hands. "Christ, Mum."

The weekend is meant to be Quality Family Time. My parents came all the way from Adelaide. We go to yum cha, the Opera House. I keep thinking about Meedy throwing up party pies and how I never followed through on my promise to take him to the dog park. Sunday night I am making in-person inquiries at the local shelters when really I should be driving Mum and Dad to the airport, and Phil has an improv thing so he won't be back till nine. Mum tells me not to worry, they'll manage. She leaves me

at Paws for Thought Animal Home and goes to meet Dad back at
the house and collect their luggage.

"Let me know, alright, sweetie? When he turns up?"

When I get home it's 10:00 p.m. and the lights are off. The National's "Don't Swallow the Cap" is blaring through the Bluetooth
speaker. "Phil?" I say. I switch the lights on and the speaker off.
The place is empty, but the dishwasher makes a little "ta-da" noise
like it has a surprise for me, and it does, it's working. I tug it open
and steam billows out, the dishes pristine. Dad must have fixed it.
Actually the whole place looks much cleaner. I imagine my mother
scrambling to pack her suitcase and vacuum at the same time and
I can't decide who I'm most pissed at: Mum, or Phil, or myself. In
the corner of the bedroom, the dog bed has been shaken clean of
fur. I run a bath and practice holding my breath for as long as I can,
peering up through the floating black curtain of my hair.

On Flexi Friday, cutting through Hyde Park after work, I see
Archimedes on a stranger's leash. He's distinctive for a border collie: dusty brown patches instead of black, pale-blue eyes. "Archimedes!" I shout.

Meedy looks up, barks happily.

"Hey!" I yell at the stranger, lengthening my stride. He's at
least a hundred feet away, heading for the edge of the park. There's
a fountain and then some trees between us. It's a warm spring day
and several people turn to look at me, even people with earphones.
"Hey, dognapper!" My heels sink into the grass and I kick them
off. "Hey! Dog thief! Stop that guy!"

The stranger cocks his head like someone is calling him from
the opposite direction. He steps onto the footpath and turns onto
Elizabeth Street.

I run through the park calling, "Meedy! Meedy!" I can see the back of this guy's head, his dumb gray baker-boy cap disappearing into a wave of pedestrians crossing the street. I weave through the trees. By the time I reach the park's stone gate, they're gone.

"You alright, miss?" A cop in a fluoro vest and bicycle helmet is right there, lounging against the gate. He looks ridiculous, the way cops on bikes do.

"That guy, who just left? He stole my dog!"

I explain the situation, still panting. I can't describe the guy: a white male in a baker's cap. I spend a while describing what I mean by "baker's cap." I never saw his face.

"Did other people in the park witness the incident?"

"Incident?"

The cop speaks loudly, like I'm elderly or deaf. "The gentleman stole your dog."

"No—oh, that was a week ago. He didn't steal it from me just now. He went up that street."

"So you saw a man you didn't recognize walking a dog that looked like your dog."

"If you go now, I bet you could still reach him on your bike."

The cop regards me coldly. "Don't have my bike with me just now, I'm afraid."

I stare up at his helmet. He stares down at my stockinged feet. I stalk off without another word. My shoes are where I left them, tipped over in the grass like two blackout drunks.

Phil finds me at home, facedown on the bed. I relay the story numbly. "But you're sure it was Meedy?"

"I think I'd recognize my own son."

"You're cute," he says.

I flop onto my back. "He looked happy, too. He looked like he was having a really nice walk. He didn't need us." My phone rings. "Will you get that? I'm not done here."

"Hello?" Phil passes the phone to me, mouths, "It's your mum."

"You alright, sweetie?" she says. Her voice is too high and sweet. I feel like a toddler.

"I'm fine."

"You find Archimedes?"

"Yes," I say. "He's doing great."

"Oh, thank goodness. Well, I was just calling to give you my love, and to say we loved seeing you *and* Phil, and we're very proud of you, okay?"

"Thanks, Mum."

"And please pass on our thanks to Allen for letting us stay in his room. It was very neat. We were a bit flustered, heading out, so we didn't quite catch him. I hope he wasn't offended."

I sit up. "Allen?"

"We thought that must have been him in the shower when we left. I heard the water running."

"Mum, you slept in the spare room. Phil was joking about having a housemate. It's just us two."

There's a long pause on the other end of the line. Phil is giving me question-mark eyebrows. I can hear Dad's gruff voice in the background. "Must have been Phil home early," he says.

"Was Phil home early?" asks Mum.

I cover the phone. "Did you swing home Sunday evening, before Mum and Dad left?" Phil squints.

"Are you okay, Liz?" Mum sounds breathless. "What's happening?"

"Yeah, Mum," I say, uncovering the speaker. "It was just Phil, home early. He didn't realize you guys were still here. Glad you got back safe."

I hang up.

"You alright?" asks Phil.

"You weren't home early," I say. I stand and crack the bedroom blinds, stare out.

"What?"

"Sunday night. Someone broke into our place. Took a shower."

"Hold up," says Phil. He reaches out his arm, brings me back to the bed. "Slow down."

"You got home after I did," I say. "You went out for drinks after improv. You said the new member was so unfunny you were signing up for memory-editing."

"Are you sure that was Sunday?" He squints. It's like he's trying to solve a terrible math problem. "Can't have been Sunday."

"It was."

He snaps his fingers. "Jolene. You gave Jolene a spare key."

"So she broke in and took a shower without telling either of us?"

We sit there, holding our elbows. The evening's still bright. Somehow all the bedroom furniture looks too shiny, like props made for a TV show.

"It must have been me," says Phil. But he looks baffled.

"Let's get out of here," I say. "Let's go get drunk."

We go to The Clare, where one of Phil's workmates has a DJ set. The place is packed with advertising bros. I can almost see the

coke wafting from the speakers. I down two gin and tonics and
find Melinda, Brian's wife, who explains she has a baggie in her
bra, so we go to a stall together and use the lid of the toilet and my
expired Dendy Cinemas membership card. I secretly despise Melinda, but she is tolerable once we're on coke. Together we watch
the guys play pool but it is too slow, we go upstairs to dance but
the music is too weird, we go back to the ladies' for another round
and the tiles are slick fluorescent white. I befriend a butch woman
named Samia at the bathroom sink and start explaining the plot
of *The Truth About Cats & Dogs* to her.

"You just have to pretend, or like, in the world of the narrative,
I guess, we have to take it for granted that Janeane Garofalo is
fugly and undesirable because she's short, but it's a massive imagi-
native leap to make, you know? And you have to pretend that Uma
Thurman is conventionally attractive."

"The chick from *Pulp Fiction*? She's hot."

"But she's hot like an alien is hot, you know? She's like a sexy
alien?"

"I took some Molly, what about you?"

"Coke, do you want some? Hey, Melinda, are you taking a shit
or what?"

"I'm good," says Samia. "Don't worry about it."

"She's not even here. God. I've been abandoned again. Samia, I
feel like we have a real connection. Fuck. I have to find Phil." My
heart's banging in my throat. "You know someone stole my dog?"

"Who?" Samia chews her lip. Her eyelashes are so long.

"A guy named Allen stole my dog!" I grab my purse. "I have to
go find Phil!"

It's all smoke and darkness and pink and orange lights on the dance floor. Phil's jumping and ducking with Brian. I grab his hand. "I need air!"

On the patio Phil bums a cigarette from a leggy drag queen. "Do you think Brian's queer?"

"I don't have time for this!" I say. "I have to ask Mum about Allen!"

"Nope, no, no, bad plan." Phil twists the phone out of my grip. "Your makeup is everywhere, Liz, you look like a raccoon. Hey, hey come back!"

He follows me down the fire-escape stairs. I hail a cab and we clamber into the back seat. Phil tries to hug me but his T-shirt is soaked through with sweat and I push him away.

"You okay?" His eyes are huge.

"Meedy left us." I can't explain it, but I can feel it, I know it's true. I'm suspended between oracular calm and a rage I can't name. "He left us for another life."

"Liz," says Phil, but he breaks off, chews his lip. I check to see if I can keep my hand level. The city gushes through the windows and then we slow, we are home.

Inside, Phil locks the door behind us. It's too quiet.

"I can hear the fridge humming," whispers Phil.

"Why are you whispering?" I whisper back.

"I feel like there's someone here," he says in a normal voice. "Hello? Is anyone in here?"

"Jesus!" I clamp my hands over his mouth. He giggles.

"I'm kidding, I'm kidding."

The darkness is cloth-thick. Anyone could be here, a whole

crowd of people waiting behind the sofas to jump out and say SUR-PRISE. It is 2:30 a.m.

"Come with me," I say softly. "To turn the lights on."

Phil finds the hall light, then the bedroom, leaning into the room but still holding my hand, same for the spare bedroom. We check behind the couches. "I'm fine," I say to the fridge. "I'm fine, I'm paranoid, I'm fine." We sit at the tiny half table in the kitchen with a glass of water each. Phil raises his to eye level and looks through it.

"I'm not Allen," he says. "You know that, right?"

I can only stare at him. His eye is big and wobbly through the glass.

"What are we talking about right now?" I say. "Have you been playing pranks on me?"

He puts the glass down and then he laughs. "Oh, god," he says. "No. Liz, of course not."

My shoulders feel like they're trying to hug my ears. Phil folds his arms on the table and plants his forehead between them.

"It was me," he mumbles into the table. It takes me a minute to hear him. "I left the gate open. That Thursday when I left for work. That's how Meedy escaped."

"It's your fault?"

He nods.

I push my chair back. The air is too bright and the glass of the windows is so dark. It's like being inside a lightbulb. "I need to shower," I say.

"Liz," he says. "Liz, I'm so sorry, please forgive me."

The bathroom is cool and dark and quiet. I shower with the

lights off and sit on the tiled floor and fume. The sobs take me over suddenly, like I'm in shock, but I'm not in shock. Meedy is gone and it is Phil's fault, and this is awful, but I am not surprised, and this is a second awfulness, how not surprised I am. Relationships have costs, Mum says, and you have to decide what you are happy paying, what you are willing to tolerate. I don't want to be furious with Phil. I don't want to lose him on top of Meedy.

I leave the shower and walk into the kitchen streaming water all over the lino. Phil is hunched at the sink, submerged to his elbows, soap bubbles twinkling. I wrap my arms around him, pressing my chest into his back. "Leave it," I say. "Come to bed."

"I'm useless." His voice catches. "You've been doing everything."

"I haven't," I tell him. "You've been stepping up. I've noticed."

"No," he says. "I haven't."

I look over his shoulder at the window above the sink, meet his eyes in the glass. Behind us are the shadows of the kitchen furniture. A water droplet snakes down my back like a shudder.

"Leave it," I say, firmly this time. "Please."

He lets me lead him to our room. I climb into bed, still damp, turning the sheets cool and clammy. Phil shucks his clothing, turns the light out. My body is jangly, percussive. Some other self will think all this through tomorrow, feel everything tomorrow, take action tomorrow. I'll get up at nine, even if I have a hangover. I'll visit all the animal shelters again and knock on all the doors along our street. Somehow, I'll find our dog. I drift into a half sleep and wake with a jerk, feeling like I'm falling through the air, again and again. Down the hall there is the clanging of pots, the squeak of the tap, water splashing. Phil's arm is warm and heavy on my ribs. Something is wrong, some new thought is waltzing toward me slowly and elegantly. I sit up and listen. Nothing. At last, I discern the near-silent drone of the fridge. It hums on and on, busily cooling its occupants, the jam jars and olive jars and withered celery resting snug in its belly. It's so steady and quiet, I might never notice it again.

Ren Arcamone is an Australian writer. She attended the Iowa Writers' Workshop and the Clarion Science Fiction and Fantasy Writers' Workshop. Her short stories are published or forthcoming in *Gulf Coast, HEAT,* the *Washington Square Review,* and *Electric Literature*'s Recommended Reading series. She lives in Iowa City.

Editor's Note

What drew us to Patrick J. Zhou's story is its heart, honesty, and healthy dose of humor. Through Jia's internal navigation of how to present his own outward identity, we're witness to a thorough deconstruction of racial and cultural stereotypes, perceptions, and assumptions. Zhou's writing is confident, instilling a strong sense of sympathy for Jia and helping us to understand his choices at every beat. We were excited to publish this story for the conversations it might elicit, and particularly for the way it challenges stereotypes and pokes fun at them, often in the same breath. That it would be a debut short story publication only made the decision to publish easier—Zhou clearly demonstrates a promising oeuvre of writing ahead, and we're honored to have *CARVE* be but a first milestone for him.

Bridget Apfeld, Fiction Editor
CARVE

Tàidù

Patrick J. Zhou

TO TUNE OUT THE AMERICAN VOICES BEHIND HIM, Jia—his forehead leaning against the tacky smog-crusted glass of the bus window—counted the fluorescent orange bulbs as they flashed by on the concrete tunnel wall. Eighty-one. Eighty-two.

I really wish I could understand what this tour guide is saying.

I know. If they just had people who spoke better English, they'd make so much more money. Serious opportunity cost when you think about it.

For thirty minutes, a couple—the only white people who'd boarded their bus of mostly Chinese tourists—had been practically shouting every thought that crossed their mind. And, despite the obtrusive performance, Jia refused to pay them any attention. He wouldn't give them that satisfaction.

Ninety, Jia muttered to himself. Ninety-one.

Maybe communist countries don't really know how to do business. It's not in their DNA.

Jia clenched his jaw but tried to keep it still. Dr. Baum said the grinding was wearing down his molars.

I bet it's on purpose. With the Chinese controlling access to everything. I mean think about what they're doing to the Uyghurs. Maybe they don't want translators they can't trust.

———

IF THE PAIR bothered anyone else, Jia couldn't tell. Up ahead, the tour guide droned on in listless Sichuanese, his croaky voice crackling through scratchy speakers. A wisp of a woman in a yellow bucket hat kneeled on the seat in front of Jia and texted on WeChat. His seatmate, who smelled like Zhonghua cigarettes, was fast asleep. None of the forty-plus Chinese natives on this tour paid the Americans any mind at all.

It's called being triggered, Felix told him once. That's why you spiral. You should name it and be aware of it. There are tips and tricks to help manage how you're feeling.

His family was always trying to help him. Last year, Jia flew back to Boston for Thanksgiving and told his brother about the lady next to him on the plane who, after a few minutes of pleasant small talk, said that his English was really good. He wasn't quick on his feet though. He never was. Instead of telling her off, he seethed quietly for the rest of the flight, angry at himself for just saying, Thanks.

Gēge, her comment is a microaggression, Felix had said. Focusing on your breathing can help you calm down when you feel triggered.

Felix went to a liberal arts college where they talked about stuff that Jia didn't in his chemical engineering program. During exams, his brother's school would hire some company to bring puppies to the campus green for students to hold and relieve stress. Jia would just binge-watch a show on his iPad in bed until he fell asleep.

So, as the Americans yammered on behind him, he tried slow breaths. Deep breaths.

You'd think they could find some intern or college student learning English who'd do it for cheap.

His mother's advice to fix what she called his tàidù, his atti-tude, relied on scripture. She'd tell him in clunky English, Clothe yourself with compassion, kindness, humility—she'd pronounce it humi-lily—gentleness, patience.

And don't look at me like that, she'd say. It's not for anyone else or for me or even for God. Do it for yourself.

So now, he closed his eyes and imagined Jesus, preaching the Sermon on the Mount, wearing a windbreaker. A holy windbreaker of patience. The very same Nike windbreaker Jia had on.

Learning English is such a good skill to have for young people in foreign countries.

Oh, he had to look at these fuckers now.

The two sat in the very back of the bus and were altogether unsurprising. The man had a crew cut and a strong straight nose. A perfectly manicured beard and sharp jaw taunted Jia's round and patchy chin. The woman had a tight blond bun, bright eyes, and an even tan. A petite frame with five-days-a-week-yoga energy. Conventionally attractive, both of them, and Instagram ready, as if any of that mattered.

But, of course it did. Not a crease of discomfort on their faces. They looked like they were ready to be anywhere; they got to be-long everywhere.

Jia panicked when he let his gaze linger too long, afraid he'd been spotted. When the Americans made eye contact, however, they smiled back with polite vacancy, a total absence of familiarity of any kind. Then they went back to complaining to each other.

Relieved, Jia went back to the tunnel's carousel of lights.

One.

Two.

Suddenly, the orange lights and the lifeless gray walls vanished. Natural light and a chorus of *whaaa*s filled the decades-old bus as they emerged onto a narrow road along a ridge. The tour guide hollered into his mic and pointed eagerly out the windows to the landscape before them—

A pristine azure sky. Hugging the mountain range as far as Jia could see, a leafy quilt of emerald, canary yellow, and red. Tall trees in the valley bowing to gusts like worshippers to a throne. A glassy pearl of a lake gleaming in the late afternoon sun. A paradise. Here it was, the great natural wonder of the Middle Kingdom, the pride of his father's province.

Jia's dad had long dreamed of bringing the whole family out here for a visit. And now, because the company needed someone to inspect a new facility in Chengdu, Jia had the chance to realize that dream for himself. He pressed his phone up against that window and took photos. He reached his hand over the small gap at the top of the window to feel the breeze. He wanted to soak in as much detail as he could. With as little distraction as possible.

Can you say something, babe? Just to ask if he can speak up and try some English more often? We might as well get something out of this.

Excuse me? The man practically yodeled it. Excuse me? This time, everyone on the bus stopped what they were doing. Jia even saw the driver tilt his head up at the rearview mirror. They all looked at the American who, with the conceit of both a paying customer and a U.S. national, draped a shameless smile across his face.

In an attempt to do right by his family though, Jia turned away from the spectacle. He put his earbuds in and pulled his phone out of the fraying polyester jacket's pocket, careful not to jostle his passport. He scrolled through his music to his "Chill Folk" playlist, put it on blast, and focused on his breathing.

This is a track jacket of humility, he thought, with a deep breath out, in rhythm with the soft plucky acoustic guitar coming on.

A track jacket of humi-lily.

THE TOUR GUIDE, who told their group to call him Dàgē (Mandarin for older brother), stood at the front of the overlook, closest to the waterfall, where a cascade of white ribbons streamed down glistening tawny rock. Jia, however, hovered at the back of the crowd, near the Americans. They were reading from Wikipedia on their phones.

Hm, this is called the White Pearl Waterfall.

Yeah, one of the widest waterfalls in the world.

The problem was that Dàgē's Mandarin didn't sound like Jia's Beijing-born maternal grandparents or what the Boston Chinese Language Sunday School taught him from first to eighth grade. Even if Jia could make out the dialect, he knew only basic vocabulary for the home, like when his wàipó and wàigōng would ask him what he wanted to eat or when his parents would fight about money in the other room. So, he knew he would take this secret to the grave: that he had to learn about his ancestral homeland by eavesdropping on some randos dictating the internet.

As best as Jia could tell, the man's name was Babe; the woman's, Baby. They were from Maryland and had a dog, cat, or child back home whom they often referred to as the Tiny Baby. While the group followed Dàgē throughout the natural preserve—by the lake so clear you could see to the bottom (*It's called Arrow Lake*) or through the woods with the golden canopy (*The yellow leaves have medicinal properties*)—no matter how their tourist amoeba was configured, Jia never drifted too far from the Americans.

What he hated even more than his stalking was that Babe's and Baby's manners were not altogether unwelcome. They weren't physically pushy and didn't crowd others like many of the Chinese did. They didn't pick their nose. They didn't spit. They had boundaries. Familiar boundaries. And, despite their performance on the bus earlier, they were whispering now. Like they did in fact remember to bring their tact but had just forgotten to unpack it.

I do wish we could ask some questions. Do you think he understood what you were asking for on the bus?

I think so. Maybe he'll get us an earpiece thing at the first stop? Oh, look at this. These trees with the berries are yews.

Babe. Yew is what Voldemort's wand is made of. She whispered "Voldemort" softly as if he still must not be named. Jia had to stifle a laugh with a fake cough.

You know, Baby, on the bright side, we're on the same tour the Chinese are taking, not just a tour catered to English speakers. It's more real, more authentic, if you look at it that way.

JIA HATED THE A-word. In college, after late nights of partying, his roommates would order takeout from the nearby twenty-four-hour Chinese place and one of his buddies would always preface the call, a palm over the speaker while the order was being repeated back, with Sorry, I know Lucky Eddie's isn't authentic. Like Jia knew how to judge what was authentic. He was two years old when he came to the states and grew up in Reading, behind both the bowling alley and his favorite spot for cheesy breadsticks, Papa Gino's. How much more authentic could he be than Lucky Eddie?

By sunset, the group arrived at a concrete plaza on the side of a mountain. There was a small building for restrooms and a cluster of stands where vendors sold meats on sticks and knockoff Peppa Pig kitsch. The tour bus, which had dropped them off back at the waterfall and had everyone's luggage, was idling in a small parking lot. The driver napped at the wheel.

At the entrance, Dàgē said that the group would have an hour to walk around, go to the bathroom, or grab a snack at one of the food stands. After this, they'd make the two-hour drive to the hotel, which would be their home base for the rest of the trip. He even repeated the instructions in choppy but serviceable English. He then left to go talk to a gaggle of other tour guides.

Jia bought some niúròugān from a stand and sat on a stone ledge overlooking an iridescent valley, awash in the wan orange dusk, eating his beef on a skewer.

The panorama looked a lot like when their family would go up to the White Mountains to see the foliage. He didn't appreciate it then. As a child, he was embarrassed when they would stop to take so many photos, hypersensitive that Americans would see their family as stereotypical Asians. Or that, when they were hiking, they'd talk too excitedly, too loudly in Mandarin, and he was afraid other families nearby would assume that they hadn't bothered to learn English. He never could stop and just enjoy the damn family time.

A few years ago, when his father was near the end, his mother brought one of their old family photo albums to the hospital. Perusing them one afternoon on the vinyl recliner by his dad's bed, Jia saw pictures of himself wearing a stiff smile on all kinds of trips—on hikes, at the beach, in Disney World—but he had no memory of these trips at all. There were so many places his parents had taken them, so many memories that Jia couldn't recall even with the evidence in front of him. It was like his childhood had been wiped, like a wet cloth over a chalkboard, replaced by a lifelong script of constant worrying, of persistent triggering, by this bad tàidù of his.

He wasn't a child anymore though. Now, he had this vista all to himself and his parents and their hollering weren't around to blame. He also looked like everyone here. He could (almost) talk like them, too. Yet, none of it felt like he thought it would. What should connection to the homeland—and the strangers that occupy it—even feel like? This was supposed to be it.

Jia looked around at the other Chinese milling about on the plaza and wondered if they even thought about things like that. Maybe that was the real privilege. Maybe they never wondered where home was, never worried about where else they could or should be.

A commotion stirred behind Jia. First, indiscriminate shouting in Mandarin. Then in American English in what sounded like Babe's voice. Of course. Jia took the last bite of his meat stick and went toward the noise.

In the main part of the plaza, in the center of all the kiosks, a crowd gathered around four people like a dance circle at a wedding: Babe and Baby on one side, and Dàgē with another Chinese man on the other.

No, we're not paying him, we didn't ask for another tour. Babe pointed to the new person who had a scowl on his face and a fanny pack on his hip.

We don't have the money, Baby pleaded. We can't afford another thing. Please.

No, no. Zhè bù xíng. Nǐ zài piàn wǒ, Dàgē shouted. You ask, I bring the friend, you pay.

Based on what Jia could understand, Dàgē had misinterpreted the couple's request on the bus. He thought that when they asked for more English to be spoken, they were asking for a separate private tour. The man next to Dàgē was apparently that new private tour guide but, based on his silence in this debate, it did not seem like his English was any better than Dàgē's. The problem was that this new guide had driven out here from a nearby village just for them. And now, he thought the Americans were backing out of their request and refusing to pay despite all his trouble coming out here. It cost gas. It cost time. It cost business. He wanted to get paid. Dàgē was threatening not to take the pair back on the bus without compensation for his friend.

The Americans were getting desperate. Babe explained that they were both just schoolteachers and were traveling on a tight budget. They were gifted a voucher for this trip by some friends from study abroad. He flipped both jeans pockets inside out and shook the limp linty cloth. Look. We. Don't. Have. Any. More. Money. That's not what I asked for, Babe spat. He wagged his finger at the two grown men. Can. You. Not. Under. Stand. Me?

Jia couldn't tell if the Chinese could understand their story. They clearly didn't believe that these two could possibly be short on cash. Dàgē shook an angry fist at Babe and Baby and pointed at a taxicab in the lot, as if banishing them to the even shantier vehicle.

Even if he wanted to help, Jia's spoken Mandarin wasn't that good. What if he accidentally made it worse? And, while the Chinese were being a little unreasonable, he also didn't know if he should believe the couple's story. What if they really could afford it and it was just a ruse to backtrack out of their obnoxious request in the first place? It was so like the rich to penny-pinch when it came to paying people they considered beneath them. This poor guy came all this way from his village to help. Plus, look at them. Was it really going to hurt them in the long run to throw this guy a few hundred yuan? They don't just get to be in a place and feel like it owes them anything.

Please, please. Baby's voice faltered under the shouts of the men who talked past and down to one another. This was just a misunderstanding, she trembled. We're really, really sorry.

She turned to the cloud of witnesses around her, some of whom had their phones out, recording this shit show. Can anyone help us here? Please, anyone? She clasped her hands, now bloodless pale, the panic electric in her eyes, begging. Her gaze fell squarely on Jia, whom she surely recognized as having lurked near them for most of the day, an apparent ally, and stepped toward him. Please, somebody?

It was true that the Chinese could be real assholes to tourists. Especially Americans. The state-controlled media didn't do American travelers any favors either, especially given the state of the relationship between the two countries. (A few years ago, when his mom took him and Felix back to visit her hometown, she told them to tell locals that they were visiting from Germany.) What if these two IG-sexy schoolteachers were telling the truth? After all, they weren't unlike so many people he'd met before, who did nothing wrong to him personally and who didn't even know they were being offensive. A little ignorant, sure, but didn't they deserve help, just as he would want help in their situation? Do unto others as they would do unto you or something?

His mother would want him to be compassionate.

His brother would tell him to self-care first.

Jia said nothing. He returned the same vacant look that they'd given him earlier on the bus. For once, he was just another black-haired, smushed-nosed, slanty-eyed, flat Chinese face in the crowd.

Then, someone from behind Jia gently pushed him aside. It was the woman with the yellow bucket hat from his bus. She scrambled into the circle between the two factions and held up both hands like she was directing traffic. She explained to Dàgē and his friend in Mandarin what the Americans had been saying. She even whipped out her phone and offered to pay them half of what they wanted. Realizing this was going to be the best they were going to get, the two Chinese relented and the new tour guide left. Dàgē cooled down, shouted hǎode, wǒmen zǒuba, and waved everyone back to the bus.

Jia stayed behind and pretended to text on his phone while people milled about. The Americans were shell-shocked yet relieved, deeply appreciative of the woman. He swore he saw Baby even briefly put her hands together and bow slightly, as she said thank you, thank you.

No worries, the woman in the bucket hat said, with a British-sounding accent. The language barrier can be hard in the more rural areas. When I heard a row, I came as soon as I could. Registering the surprise on their two faces, she explained, Oh, I lived in Sydney for secondary school and uni. I do love meeting Americans. *Friends* is my favorite program.

OTHER THAN THE wind whistling over the engine's mechanical churn, their bus was silent on the way to the hotel. A moonless night sheathed the mountains and their proud long-standing trees in black velvet. And, through that window, Jia saw nothing that indicated that this place, on the other side of the world, was where he came from. There were no roots here.

Worse still, his mother would have been ashamed of him. He should have helped Babe and Baby. Sure, his Mandarin wasn't perfect, but he knew enough and could say enough. It would have been the decent thing to do. His one solace was that, for the first time, he blended in with the crowd. His shame, rather than being shouted on the mountainside, could go unnoticed, faceless and unknown. Just like he always wanted. Exhausted and spent, Jia pulled out his music again, put in his earbuds, and fell asleep.

When they arrived at the hotel, their group was exhausted. The bus itself wheezed and sputtered as they parked like it too needed a good night's sleep. Eyelids hung heavy as they trudged off. Limp necks and slumped shoulders waited for luggage. Everyone smelled like sweat.

Jia's suitcase came out first, so he led the group's walk through the fluorescently lit lobby. Dàgē, who was already there at the front desk talking to the night manager, told everyone to get out their IDs to turn in, as was protocol for travelers. But when Jia got there, he reached for his jacket pocket and found only his phone. His passport was gone.

He patted his jeans pockets, knowing full well that it didn't even fit there. Could he have left it at the overlook? Or dropped it in the pond? Did he lose it over the ledge he had sat on? Or in the plaza? Dàgē had said this cluster of hotels was the only visitor lodging for hours; on the off-chance that anyone did pick it up somewhere, at the very least he wasn't getting it back tonight. But forget being able to check into this hotel—he had no other identification with him. If he didn't find it, how would he get home?

As he stood there, repeatedly patting his body in empty places where there weren't even pockets, he began to hyperventilate. In front of Dàgē, the desk clerk, and his group, the heat in his chest bubbled, hot and fast. His windbreaker was a straitjacket.

Then, Jia got a tap on his shoulder. It was Babe. Picked this up on the floor of the bus. Thought it was ours. He held out his hand in which was firmly clamped, between his index finger and thumb, Jia's passport in its navy-blue glory with the "United States of America" emblazoned in gold foil.

Also, I think these are yours, too. In his other hand were Jia's earbuds. He hadn't even noticed they'd fallen out.

Unable to look the man in the face, all Jia could muster was a weak confession, the one thing he could think of saying on the spot while accepting his items from this man.

Sank you. Like he was Mickey Rooney in *Breakfast at Tiffany's*.

The same shame he felt back then—on those mountain hikes in the autumn, when his mom and dad would chitchat and laugh and point and *whaaa* with such unfettered joy for the beauty in their newly adopted home, when he, at eleven years old, would chastise them for how they were embarrassing him when they made such a scene in public—it all wound tightly around him now. It was all the same yoke.

He turned to the hotel clerk and spoke hurriedly in Mandarin, asking for the opening times for the hotel restaurant. Like reverting back quickly to the foreign language could cover up what'd been exposed, as if he could make it sound like, despite having a U.S. passport, his English still wasn't very good.

Nidecantingshenmeshihoukaimen?

The clerk furrowed his brow and looked confused. Wǒ méi tīngdǒng. He paused before adding, Wǒyě huì shuō yīngyǔ.

No way in hell Jia was going to speak English to this man. He tried again, more slowly this time, sure to enunciate his tones carefully.

O, míngbáile, the clerk said to Jia's clammy relief. The restaurant opened for breakfast at 6:00 a.m.

Like Jia would ever leave his room and present his sorry face in public again.

Once he got his room key card, he scurried away from the throng, their mute gazes on his back. His luggage wheels tumbled loudly over the lobby floor, squealing because they didn't line up properly. But he couldn't fix them. He couldn't afford to stop. The last Jia overheard from the now distant group behind him—the last he wanted to hear from them—was that springy Australian accent and his two compatriots.

That was quite kind of you.

Oh, it's nothing really. Treat others as you'd want to be treated, I always say.

Why don't you have breakfast with us in the morning? Our treat . . .

Unable to stand the idea of waiting in the elevator with anyone else, Jia headed straight for the stairwell despite his fifth-floor room. He lugged and banged that suitcase up the endless flight of concrete steps, under the flickering light of failing yellow bulbs, knowing that everyone, the Chinese, the Americans, could see him, would always see him wherever he went, wherever he'd go.

Patrick J. Zhou was born in China but raised in the Boston area. He works at the FDA and lives in Washington, D.C., with his wife Joy and their cat Bobby Newport.

Editor's Note

Former *Cincinnati Review* fiction editor Brock Clarke concludes his essay "The Case for Meanness in Fiction," from the book *I, Grape*, with this note: "[This] should illuminate something for us fiction writers: that the world, with its demands that in our fiction we be good, that we be nice, that we be kind, that we be compassionate, that we devote ourselves to the beauty of the *human heart*, makes it difficult for us to see that our job as fiction writers is, not to be mean for meanness' sake, but rather to find ways to be honest about how very difficult it is to be good." Faire Holliday's "Standing Still" provides a bracing and delightful example of what Clarke means. It's the portrait of a complicated young woman who—the better angels of her nature having abandoned her, possibly to dance on the head of a pin—is doing the flawed, ragged, selfish best she can. Some writers see an alluring safety in setting one's stories in a world that's been morally childproofed for our and its characters' protection, a world where everyone is impeccably right-minded, right-hearted. Holliday resists that, to her story's great benefit and to the reader's. This is a story with plenty of sharp edges on which to cut ourselves.

Michael Griffith, Fiction Editor
The Cincinnati Review

Standing Still

Faire Holliday

Just enough

LUIS KNOWS I'M NOT IN LOVE WITH HIM, ALTHOUGH he's never asked. I can tell by the way he fits himself around the space where the question would go, always aware of the outline of it, the sharp edges that would catch and cut him if he got too close. Some days I wish he would put words to it, so we could build something on that truth or move on with our lives. Other times I'm thankful for the omission. Until the question is asked, until it's answered, we can exist in the balance of just enough. Just enough companionship. Just enough affection. Just enough in common to make it through the long, lonely afternoons of youth's end.

He's nine years older than me, divorced, and father to a young son named Ant who calls me Ms. Seneca. Ant splits his time between his maternal grandmother's house and Luis's, a situation that no one seems to particularly like. I asked Luis about it once, and the only thing he said was "The boy needs some kind of mother."

The arrangement is unofficial. Ant goes where he goes based on everyone's work schedules. It's the sort of situation that Luis could easily use to his advantage, ghosting away under the pretense of longer shifts. He hasn't, though. Ant comes over a few nights a week and takes up the corner of the living room with the spare bed. From his small backpack, an explosion of things pours forth. Notebooks, shoes, toys, clothes. Doritos crumbs, like a flaming comet tail across the tan sheets. Within five minutes he's nested so thoroughly that it's hard to imagine the space without him there.

I don't usually stay long on these nights because Ant makes me uncomfortable. His presence introduces an element of uncertainty about who is central and who is peripheral. It's less complicated for all of us if I just find somewhere else to be.

Tourism

Luis drives a delivery van for a local mattress shop. All day long he carries mattresses in and out of houses. Up and down stairs, through doorways that are too small. Around cracked paving stones and angry dogs and overturned bicycles. He sees inside so many houses that the novelty is gone. It's rare that anything shocks him. Dirt, filth, neurotic cleanliness. Women who see the color of his skin and clutch their cell phones until he's gone. Men who bark commands as if he were a clumsy child, saying things like "Carefully, carefully. Stop, stop, stop. You need to watch where you're going, son." As if he hadn't wrestled hundreds of mattresses around people's valuables in the last five years.

"What have you learned from it?" I asked him, the first time he talked about finding a different job.

"That poor people tip better than rich people," he said. "And that most people own way too much shit."

I work for an upscale neighborhood grocery store, one of those places where you can get homemade beeswax candles and organic bok choy along with your toilet paper and condoms. If Luis asked me what I've learned from it, I'd say: "That I'm afraid of the unidirectional nature of success."

Not that exactly. Those words have come only after years of contemplation, and they sound pretentious even in my own head. What I'd really say is that I'm afraid to move on, afraid to get a professional job. I'm afraid the added responsibilities will weigh too heavily on me. That once I step onto that treadmill of professionalism, I won't ever step off. I'll jog along in place, pulled ever onward by the reward of retirement. I'll stop living and start wanting.

And yet I'm aware of the liminal space I exist in. I lurk on the edges of poverty. I'm a visitor on those gritty shores. I've got a college degree and parents with connections. Upward mobility is not an impossibility if I'm willing to compromise for it. If there's one thing Luis has taught me, it's that poverty is a different ball game when you know you'll never escape. All those things that give me a sense of freedom are crushing weights to him.

"I will never work in a cubicle," I said one day, as we watched people coming out of downtown offices at the beginning of the lunch hour.

"Me either," he said, studying the calluses on his hands.

A statement of rebellion for me. A statement of fact for him.

Stick figures

Sometimes I wonder if I'd be in love with Luis if it weren't for Ant. I sense that Ant wonders it too. I read it in his face the first time I met him, a feeling of being unwanted that you could almost see in his features. I thought about the nine-year-old I had been, all fat cheeks and loud voice and unabashed self-promotion. It took me until the end of grade school to learn that the world didn't cater to my whims. Ant must have been born with this knowledge.

Perhaps because of this, Ant exists carefully within himself. Sometimes he just sits and stares out the window for long stretches of time. Or watches whoever happens to be in the house, his face devoid of expression.

"You okay, bud?" I asked him, the first time this happened. Luis had been called into work unexpectedly, so we'd been left alone together.

"Antony," he said. No resentment or petulance. Just a neutral statement.

"Are you okay, Antony?" I asked.

"Yes," he said, not breaking his stare.

I went back to my phone, thinking about all the passive-aggressive things adults say to children in these types of situations. *Don't you know it's rude to stare? Didn't your parents teach you manners?* In the end I just looked up from my phone again and stared back. For almost five minutes, we sat looking at each other. I couldn't manage eye contact for that long, so I looked at his nose and the curve of his jaw, mostly. The air around his head. His pudgy hand resting on the windowsill. He stared at me without any of the same self-consciousness. I broke first, plunging my eyes back to the safety of my phone screen.

Months later he stopped looking at me altogether. That was almost as disconcerting. I'd ask him something, and he'd keep his eyes averted as he answered. It made me wonder if he'd been looking for something in particular and was conveying his disappointment about not finding it. What was he looking for, though? A maternal instinct? The promise of kindness? Beauty? Intelligence?

"I think he's just fascinated with faces," Luis said when I asked. "He's been that way since he was a kid."

The next time Ant came over, I waited until he was in the bathroom and then snooped through the notebooks on his bed. I was hoping to find my face rendered in incredible detail on one of those pages or at least some suggestion of savant-like talent. Anything that could provide an explanation for his staring. I found the sort of scribbles and doodles you'd expect from any nine-year-old. Stick figures and boxy cars. Disembodied eyes. A spiral that went on and on across the spine of the notebook.

I put everything back in its place before he caught me.

Mustard

On the rare occasions Luis, Ant, and I are in public together, I often pretend we're a happy family. I can't explain why except for a deeply instilled belief that you have to hide dysfunction from others. I lean forward when Ant speaks, acting as if I were raptly interested in the things he's saying. I laugh at his jokes. I offer to buy him things. Ant's too smart not to recognize the charade. Life has made him keenly aware of all the stages of rejection, even the ones that look like affection.

There are limits to the performance, of course. Once, sitting outside a hot-dog stand downtown, I caught myself in the act of reaching toward Ant to wipe mustard off his chin. It was an innocuous gesture, really, but it felt so motherly that I couldn't bring myself to do it. I couldn't bear to have him pull his face back from my hand or, worse, bury it in Luis's shoulder, that yellow glob smearing into the worn fabric of his father's T-shirt. I couldn't stand to see him undo my careful lie of domestic tranquility.

I pulled my hand back and muttered something to Ant about the mustard smear. He left it there for the rest of the evening. Eventually his dad scratched it off with a fingernail before we all got in the car to go home.

Sex

My favorite times with Luis are when we're alone together in the evenings, sitting out on his porch and watching the world go by. He lives in the basement of an old house that's been broken into apartments. The porch is communal space, so we're never guaranteed to be alone. I savor those times when it's just the two of us. In the summer the heat lingers around us like tangible desire. I can't be in his presence for too long without wanting him to lead me down the long stairway to his bedroom. *This is our conversation,* I think, as he peels off my clothing. This is the way we tell each other about our days, in the pace and tenor of our lovemaking.

Afterward, he talks. It's always dim in his apartment, so I can't see his face. I stare at the ceiling and imagine his features—his large dark eyes and heavy brow, a slightly hooked nose, soft lips, and a chin that falls a little too quickly away to neck. It's an attractive face, rendered even more so in my visualization of it during those soft moments in his bed, our mingled sweat cooling on us. Sometimes my mental image of him will be so strong that I'm shocked when I finally see his real features again.

I wonder if he does that to me: edits my face when he's not looking at me. Gives me straighter teeth and eyes that are a little wider apart. Fixes all the things in my most self-abrasive thoughts. Maybe he makes me beautiful, undeniably beautiful.

What would I give to live confidently in either attractiveness or ugliness? On the back of Luis's motorcycle, I wish idly for a gentle crash, a slide across the pavement that would tear up the skin of my face, just so I would finally know for sure. Just so I could stop wondering. It's not a real wish. It's not a hankering for self-mutilation. On all but my worst days, I exist in an uneasy truce with the uncertainty. I just wish I knew, when Luis or another man looked at me, what they really saw.

When Luis is done talking, we shower and make dinner. We turn on the lights, and sometimes in that harsh fluorescence, our thoughts curdle into complaints about bosses and housemates and friends. It's as if there isn't enough goodness in the world to discuss for an entire evening. Eventually we have to move on to the things that hurt us. As we talk, Luis's relaxed body will tighten slowly, like someone is cranking a wrench. One click, his jaw clenches. Two clicks, his back grows rigid. Three clicks, his palms clench and unclench, spreading veins across his arms like lightning.

Flying

This is what it's like to be on the back of Luis's motorcycle: free. Freer than I've ever been. The motorcycle is old and barely gets to speeds above fifty. We take back roads instead of highways wherever we're going. Luis complains about how slow the bike is, but all I know is that it's faster than my anxieties. For those thirty minutes as we zoom, fluid, through the air, my mind stops racing. My chest opens up and I breathe deeply. The helmet clenches my head, the thickness of Luis's old leather jacket smothers me, but I feel strangely weightless. I feel lifted outside of myself.

I used to think middle-aged men on motorcycles were laughable. I thought it was about chasing youth, about trying to reclaim a spot among the reckless. Now I understand that it's more than that. It's about striving to be greater than the sum of what you watch and eat and fear and crave. It's about feeling that life is still full of possibilities, not just doors to rooms you've already been in.

It's a lie in motion, I guess.

Stagnancy

Luis commits to things. Not often, but more often than me. He was married once, to Ant's mother. He stood in the front of a church and committed to spending his life with one other human. He committed to having Ant, not before he was conceived, but afterward, when he and his wife decided whether to keep him. And after that, when his wife left, Luis committed to still being present for Ant. He committed to having a job that would let him buy the things his son needs to fit in at elementary school: new clothes, nice sneakers, a tablet, Lunchables. The sort of accessories that allow even a kid like Ant to fly under the radar.

What have I committed to? Luis asks me this often, directly and indirectly. It's one of those arguments that we spin around and around in our hands, trying to mold into something. It never really changes, though. We never really change.

"Friends," I say. "I've committed to my friends."

Abbie and Christa and Emmaline and Sutter. Friends from high school and college. Friends who ask nothing of me except to be available sometimes to listen and drink with them. That's the sort of commitment that doesn't take anything from you, and Luis knows this. He's not satisfied with the answer.

"My job," I tell him. It's not true, but it should be. It's a nice enough place to work. The pay is terrible, but the hours are decent, and I'm not exhausted at the end of the day. I've been there long enough that a lot of customers know me by name and think we're friends. I should love that, I guess. I'm a fixture in the community. A few months ago a kid saw me out and about and called me "the co-op lady." For just a moment I thought I could lean into it, but then I realized that a nickname like that means you've been somewhere too long. And so I spend hours in the evening scrolling through Craigslist, looking for new beginnings. I can't abide the thought of standing still.

"Relationships, Seneca," Luis always says, at a certain point in the commitment conversation. "I'm talking about whether you've ever committed to a romantic relationship."

He knows the answer. I've told him about everyone I've dated. He was interested—jealous—and I like lists. (One) Warren, in high school. Wasn't too much going on upstairs, but he had nice hands and a car that we'd drive in for hours. (Two) Sam, freshman year of college. Two months of drunken sex in our dorm rooms when our roommates were out. My first pregnancy scare. (Three) AJ, sophomore year of college. Talked too much. Wore polos tucked into chinos and made backhanded comments about my mom for months after he briefly met her. (Four, five, six) Ryan, Matty, Nikola. Booty calls, really. One of them used to cry at war movies,

but I can't remember which one. (Seven) Marcus. Broke my heart.
(Eight) James. We ruined a perfectly good friendship trying to date.
(Nine) Luis.

Luis always homes in on Marcus, but I tell him that it doesn't
matter much. He's just the only person who ever really got to me.

I'm only the second woman Luis has dated since his divorce.
The first, Stella, was a classic rebound. They were engaged after
only two months of dating, and they muddled through another
year and a half before realizing it was a mistake. He and I have
been together for almost as long. Only once did he say anything
about those comparable timelines that really meant something.

"Sometimes I think I'm the only one in the world looking for
something serious," he said before I left one evening. I'd been
talking about moving, traveling, changing—doing something
other than standing still. I hadn't realized how thoughtless it
was, telling him about all my plans to live without him. I guess
I didn't really think he'd care. No, that's a lie. Honestly, I just
didn't think about it. When he said that, I felt everything folding
in on itself.

"Oh," I said.

"Yeah," he said, laughing painfully. "I know what you're really
saying."

That was almost six months ago. I don't know if I'd still be with
him if he hadn't said that. Guilt is a powerful immobilizer.

Impermanence

My friend Abbie, who's married now, told me once that she never
dated anyone she couldn't see marrying.

"What's the point, Seneca?" she asked me. "How can you enjoy something you know will end eventually?"

"How can you enjoy something you know won't end?" I asked.

She laughed a little until she realized I was serious. We never talked about it again.

Friends

Abbie knows about Luis, but she's the only one. When I'm out with other friends, I don't mention him by name. I don't even acknowledge having a boyfriend. Stories about Luis become about "a friend." He blurs into everyone else in my life. You would realize he's a common thread only if you were paying really close attention.

Abbie knows about him by accident. My car died when I was over at her house one time. It was still a few days away from payday. Calling Luis was my only option. He came right away, even though he was helping one of his friends move. This was early in the relationship, when gestures like that seemed important. He showed up in Abbie's neighborhood on his raspy motorcycle, blasting '90s hip-hop. He was wearing a white undershirt covered in dirt and sweat from carrying boxes all day. Seeing him standing on Abbie's pathway, in between two well-manicured rose bushes, I felt a deep-down flicker of shame, like I'd broken some unspoken rule by bringing him there. After I saw that Abbie was warming to him, the feeling faded but didn't completely go away. A few of Abbie's neighbors drove by, slowing way down when they saw him working on my junky car. I should have been infuriated by those looks, by that clear demarcation of otherness. Instead I felt a desire to somehow show myself as one of them, to cross that invisible line separating people who belonged in the neighborhood and people who didn't.

Now, sixteen months later, I erase Luis's existence from my life in all the stories I tell my friends. I tell myself that it's what I'd be doing in any relationship nearing its end, but I wonder. And I do really like Luis. That's the complicated part. I like the feel of his callused hands on my skin, the smell of him. I like how he fixes things with spare parts from other things: washing-machine belts, bed frames, pedals from exercise bikes, old faucet handles, even the insides of a gumball machine. I like the way he thinks, so different from anyone else I know. That he sings without realizing it when he's lost in a task. Most of all, I like that he isn't like the people I grew up with, how dating him sets me apart from all of them. How I'll never have neatly tended roses if I stay with him.

But none of these things can feed love, raise it from a helpless infant to something that can stand on its own.

The beginning

"You don't like my dad much," Ant says one day when we've been left alone together. Luis needs a root canal and has been picking up all the extra shifts he can get. This is the sixth afternoon in a row I've been stuck with babysitting duties, and I'm getting really tired of it.

"What?" I say. It's the first time I can remember him initiating a conversation with me.

"I can tell," he says. "Ms. Stella used to look at him the same way near the end."

"You don't know what you're talking about," I say, looking back at my phone. I'd hide my face if I could. Now that I know Ant can read me like that, I feel unsettled, naked. Every twitch of my mouth feels like a broadcast of my deepest thoughts.

"Are you going to marry my dad?" he asks.

I sigh and look up at him with exaggerated slowness, as if the question were unbearably heavy. It strikes me that he's chosen to look at me again, after all those months of looking away. *To hell with it*, I think. *If this is how it ends, at least I can get out of babysitting.*

"No," I say.

"I didn't think so."

We both go back to doing our own things. He stares out the window. I scroll through Twitter without really seeing anything. After a few minutes I get up and go to the bathroom. I stare at myself in the mirror and pretend I'm talking to Luis. I look at what my features do, and try to find which one betrays me. My eyes in the mirror look old and hard, surrounded by little wrinkles I swear weren't there before. There's a flicker of movement in the mirror. I glance over my shoulder to find Ant watching me through the crack in the door.

"See?" he says.

Later that night I lie in Luis's bed and stare at the ceiling. My whole body feels strung tightly. I jump at every little floor creak.

"Does Ant see a counselor?" I ask.

I'm pretty sure Luis is asleep. A few long seconds go by, and then he mumbles, "My kid's not crazy."

"It could be good for him. Give him someone to talk to about his feelings."

"He's a kid. What feelings could he possibly need to talk about?"

"I don't know," I say. "Loneliness, sadness. That sort of thing. He's been through a lot."

Luis lets out a snort. "If he can't handle those feelings at age nine, he's in for a rude awakening," he says.

"I'm worried about him," I say. Even as the words leave my mouth, though, I realize it's not true. What's keeping me awake isn't worry about Ant. It's the unsettled feeling that he knows a secret I was sure I was hiding.

Frog

Luis and I take a trip to the coast on his motorcycle, pulling off on the shoulder every time a fast truck comes up behind us. The two-hour trip takes almost four hours this way, but neither of us minds.

Ant stays home with his grandmother. He texts a picture of a squashed frog he found on the pavement outside.

"My strange son," Luis says, showing me the photo and laughing.

"Does he have friends?" I ask.

Luis shrugs and tucks the phone back into his pocket. We ride on until we get to our motel. It's all gray wood and rusted handrails, but the linens are clean and the door locks behind us. We don't leave the room again until it's fully dark outside. In the restaurant Luis strokes the inside of my thigh with his work-roughened thumb, and I let myself simply enjoy being with him.

It's the perfect evening. Somehow, it seems to encapsulate the entirety of our relationship, like that old saying about the universe being contained in a grain of sand. Lying sleepless in bed hours later, I realize that this is the beginning of the end. There's something too good about this day, as if we've reached the crest of our relationship and have nowhere to go but down.

We leave early the next morning to get Luis home in time for work. As the silhouettes of the trees slip past in the predawn light, I wrap my arms tightly around his waist and press the side of my helmet into his back, pretending we're still lying in bed together.

Knowledge

"Maybe we should get to know each other," I say to Ant the next time we're by ourselves.

"Why?" he asks.

"It seems like a good idea," I say.

"Do you actually care?"

"Yes," I say, surprised to find that it's true. Or, more to the point, I'm interested in finding out how a nine-year-old can read me like no one else can. Anything more than that, and I'm bound to get bored.

"Weird, but okay," Ant says, making a face.

We stare at each other for a while. I try to think of normal questions to ask a kid. Is it like getting to know someone on a first date? Or is there more subtlety to it than that?

"What do you like to do?" I ask.

"What do you like to do?" he counters.

I think of all the lies I've told men over the years, the unbounded space we both exist in before our personalities take shape. How it's so much safer to answer this question second, so I can pick and choose parts of myself. *I'm just starting to get into rock climbing.*

I love reading Dostoevsky too. I'm a big fan of the craft-beer scene. If I'm lucky, the person figures out the lie gradually. All at once, and the relationship is doomed to fail. Nice and slowly, and maybe I can keep it going for a few more months. It's like letting air out of a balloon.

"I like riding on your dad's motorcycle," I say. "I like going out with friends and drinking and making fun of other people at the bar. I like scrolling through my phone until my brain feels sort of numb and heavy."

"I like finding dead things on the road," Ant says. "I think it looks really cool when they are squished and their organs are coming out."

"Do you squish them yourself?" I ask.

"Of course not," he says, looking affronted at the very idea. A little while later, he says, "I like pretending I'm rich."

"Why?" I ask.

"Because then people would like me." He shrugs.

Fantasy

I meet someone else when I'm out with friends. Brian. He sits across the table from me, and we don't talk much, but he haunts my thoughts for days afterward. I imagine the endless conversations we'll have. All the things we'll have in common. The look of arousal and wonder on his face when I undress in front of him for the first time. The ease with which he'll get along with the people I care about.

I know it's not about him, not really. It's about the potential of him. A new story. Another chance for happiness, timelessness. That endless feeling of being young and free.

Really, though, it's about believing I'll be a better person the next time around. That selfishness is just a side effect of an unfulfilling relationship, not a permanent way of being.

Park

Ant and I go to the park. Luis is a week out from the root canal, and all I can think is: *Seven more days. Seven more days.* I look over at Ant as we walk, and wonder if he's thinking the same thing.

When we're halfway there, he puts out a finger and touches the back of my hand. Quickly, furtively. Just a quick touch and then the hand is back in the pocket of his sweatshirt before I can say anything. His touch lingers on my skin, sticky with sweat and the remains of a popsicle he gobbled before we left. I feel like wiping my hand on my jeans but resist the urge. All I can think of is that flattened frog with its guts coming out. How Ant must have bent down and looked at it for a long time, inspecting it this way and that with the same silent stare he used on me when we first met. For just a moment I move outside of my own selfishness and think about what it must feel like to be that alone. Then I take a step farther away from him as we walk so he can't touch me again.

At the park I sit on the edge of a stone wall and bury my head in my phone. I don't want to engage with any of the other adults. I don't want to answer any of their questions or try to hide the fact that I don't really like kids. One of the mothers sits down a few feet away and turns her body toward me. I sense she's ready to pounce the moment I look up from my phone. I don't give her the satisfaction. After a few minutes she lets out a judgmental sigh and walks away.

Not much later, a kid starts screaming. I look up to find that one of the taller boys is bleeding from his nose, heavy droplets falling into his cupped hands. I look around, waiting for someone to come to his aid, only to find I'm one of very few adults in the vicinity. There's a father trying to slow down his daughter's swing and that mother, grappling with two squirming toddlers. I meet the mother's eyes, and she looks at me for a long moment before returning to her task. I sigh and get to my feet.

"Where's your adult?" I ask the kid.

"At home," he says, gesturing vaguely to a row of houses. I step back to avoid a splatter of blood.

I fish a tissue out of my purse and hand it to him gingerly. He grabs it and shoves it up to his nose.

"Are you going to be okay?" I ask.

"Probably," he says. "Mom always says it's not a big deal."

I look at the other two adults for help, but they've both stopped paying attention now that someone has taken charge.

"Cool," I say. We all stand there for a moment—this bleeding kid, Ant, a little blond girl who must be related to the girl on the swings, and me—then I turn and walk back to the wall.

"That's my mom," Ant says, behind me. I look up, expecting to see Natasha, his birth mother, striding toward us across the grass. I've seen pictures of her and would recognize her sharp chin anywhere. There's no one new in sight, though, and as I sit down, it hits me. He's talking about me.

"She's very pretty," the girl says.

He's talking about me.

"Yeah," Ant says, shrugging. Then he slaps a hand on her arm and says, "Tag, you're it."

And they're off again, the tall kid trying to run with one hand pressed to his face. No loss of equilibrium for any of them. Meanwhile, I feel like someone has flipped me upside down and spun me in violent circles. *Mom*, I think. The word tastes like bile in my mouth.

It happens all of a sudden, the kernel of a thought growing to a roaring voice in my head growing to an action within the space of a breath. Before I can really think it through, I'm walking away from the park. I can still hear the shrieks of Ant and his new friends on the playground. I shove my hands into the pocket of my sweatshirt and pick up the pace. *Tell Luis you blacked out for a while*, an inner voice says. *You don't know what happened.* And, a moment later, *Ant will come home on his own. He's smart.* There's no counterargument to that. Later, I'll tell myself that if I had actually thought, *Maybe he won't make it home okay*, I wouldn't have left. I would have interrupted my momentum and been able to turn. This lends credence to the blackout theory. That excuse, initially intended to get Luis off my back, becomes the only sense of self I'm able to hold on to.

Voices and faces

Home, bedroom, door closed, headphones in. The sunlight moving across my ceiling. Afternoon to evening to night.

Luis's voice on the phone saying, "Where's Ant, Seneca?"

My own voice saying, "He's not home?"

A Facebook post from Ant's grandmother: "Please help us find our angel. Antony Moreno nine y/o last seen near Farragut Park in N Portland. Wearing a gray sweatshirt & red basketball shorts."

Luis's text message saying, "PICK UP THE PHONE."

My cold face in the mirror. Eyes that I don't recognize anymore.

And then Luis, his fists thundering against my front door. My roommate coming out of her room in a T-shirt and pair of underwear, rubbing the sleep out of her eyes, asking if she should call the cops.

It's not just Luis, when I open the door. It's Luis and Ant, holding each other's hands in a death grip. Ant looks tarnished and terrified, and I think through the consequences of nine hours, what sort of horrors those can hold.

"I'm sorry," I say to him.

"You don't talk to him," Luis says, shoving Ant most of the way behind him. Ant's dark eyes peer at me from around his father's arm. I can't bear to look at them any longer.

"He called you Mom, and you walked away," Luis says.

"I don't remember . . ." I start.

"You fucking bitch," Luis says, and there's anger matching the despair in his voice. I look up to find him making a fist and imagine those knuckles flashing into my skin, the bruises blooming across my paleness. For a moment I even long for it: an act of violence that will absolve me of all I've done. I imagine the retelling of it in the years to come, my decision diminishing in contrast to his, fading into a footnote instead of the main event.

Luis's fist finds my doorframe. Wood and bone splinter simultaneously, and Luis gives a yell, tucking his hand into the crook of his elbow.

"You fucking bitch," he says again, now crouching over from the pain, taking in shaking breaths. Over his father's bent back, Ant continues to look at me, now with an expression of loneliness deeper than any I've seen. Deeper than the well that's inside of me by far.

"I'm sorry," I say to Ant again.

He shrugs and looks away.

"It's okay," he finally says.

The three of us stand there for what feels like an eternity.

"Don't ever come near my son again," Luis says, finally, standing up. His voice is quiet and resigned. He doesn't look at me again.

"Luis, Ant," I say to their retreating backs, but neither of them turns.

Moving on

There's a trick I've learned over the years, a survival skill, really, once a relationship ends. It involves reframing the narrative into something I can live with, forgetting some things and highlighting others, making it into a story I can remember with a detached sort of fondness. I eventually managed to do this with Luis, keeping the good and discarding the bad. Ant, though—Ant continues to elude me. No matter how hard I try, I can't reshape him. I can't change our story into anything else. I've always considered myself a neutral force, selfish but not inherently bad. Just someone trying to live my life the way I want. I'm not certain of it anymore, though. Doubt has crept in.

The other day, I was out with someone new, and we got on the topic of past relationships. Without thinking much about it, I launched into my usual list. I was almost to the end when my date interrupted.

"You're not obligated to tell me about everyone you've ever been with," he said, laughing.

I opened my mouth to say I didn't mind, because it felt so important at that moment to let him know that I was someone who moved on without looking back. That I was someone who lived without tethers. Outside the window, a dark-haired boy walked by with a dog. For a moment, I saw Ant's face so vividly that my heart squeezed up in my chest. It struck me then that what I was going to say about Marcus—*he was the only one who ever really got to me*—was no longer true. Now there were two.

"Sorry," I said, once the moment had passed. I looked down to find I was holding on tightly to the edge of the table. I forced a smile. "What do you want to talk about?"

"What do you like to do?" he asked.

I looked at him and considered all the possibilities, including telling the truth.

"You go first," I said.

Faire Holliday is a writer with roots in Oregon and Washington. She draws inspiration from the varied experiences she's been able to have, from working at a free restaurant for people experiencing homelessness to interning at the World Health Organization. She is the 2022 winner of the Robert and Adele Schiff Award for fiction and is currently finishing her first novel.

Editor's Note

At *Driftwood Press*, we're particularly interested in the extreme compression demanded by the short length of our fiction. In only nine pages, Alfonseca's short piece paints a family with dense specificity, a gripping voice, and colorful detail, all while utilizing an innovative structure that balances location, interiority, and time's weathering with unconventional modulation and a poetic sensibility. It's this poetic sensibility that we're so often attracted to in *Driftwood* stories—fiction writers who, as Faulkner once said of himself, are "failed poets." Alfonseca may not be a writer of poetry in the conventional sense, but she's written poetry here. The language on display pops with rhythm, with energy, surety, and conviction: "My tongue too fat inside my mouth. Words too slick for my tongue . . . Two islands on my tongue. Two Islands on my tongue." And yes, the ever-trenchant themes of American homogenization hit home here, hard: "I am now a girl from the U.S. and not the islands on my tongue." / ". . . my grandmother's one-bedroom American dream." Dailihana E. Alfonseca is handling enough threads here for a nine-pager, right? Not quite; this is that extreme compression on display. She deftly uses magical realism to bind her ideas in the tight space she's allotted herself. "Iguanas would climb into bed with us at night to whisper stories of our ancestors in our ears, messages all three of us needed to hear." "Spanish Soap Operas Killed My Mother" is one such whispered story: one you'll be whispering in your sleep, long after reading.

James McNulty, Co-Founder, Managing Fiction Editor
Driftwood Press

Spanish Soap Operas Killed My Mother

Dailihana E. Alfonseca

I. Island Gal

THERE USED TO BE MORE FAT BETWEEN THE EARTH *and my bones. Back when the palm trees swayed our family to sleep in hammocks made of plantain leaves. Way back when our homes had no glass on the windows, the air smelled vibrant and green, the walls rough with concrete like sea foam and salt water. Iguanas would climb into bed with us at night to whisper stories of our ancestors in our ears, messages all three of us needed to hear. My mother had already let the man come in. Domesticated her tongue and now she screamed and ran whenever the iguana tried to warn her of the plans of God.*

I barely remember my father. Yet I remember he links me to the Oyo Empire. The only memory I recall with him nauseates me in sweet pink and sticky sap. Strawberry sickness covers the dashboard. He is upset. I cry. He laughs. His gold chains in the Caribbean sun glint at me and trap their way into my soul. I didn't know then what I know now. About the paging of addicts needing their fix or why his fingers glistened with jewels and money that came from a war that began in opium dens to the east. All I know is that I am a glutton for excess because of him. He teaches me my first lesson. Too much of anything can only result in sickness and in death.

I remember how Mami chased Papi around with a bat after she found him bringing us home with the lady who had the same color hair as her but not her height. The cherry-red lips of his convertible busted open as she drove the bat into his car like the cigarette gently sitting on his bottom lip. While Mami chases Papi, I see Papi chasing other women.

"Do you think he feels bad?" The gum snaps between the question and the clucking of hens in the yard.

My mother's wrist now laden with my father's spoils scrapes the white grains from a bottom-heavy pot. "No, men never feel bad for anything." The pastelito with its cumin, sazón, and ground beef screams at her from the frying pan. It yells the sizzling protest of my virility and misunderstanding. Our small house is hot with tension as Mami waits up for his arrival, and when my father does not come home she thinks it is just another woman.

After his death our island stinks fragrantly of deceased sorrow as we board an avian boat toward the broken sea of opportunity.

We arrive with one suitcase and no English to our name. My grandmother is already in the mainland of success. Abuela is not as domineering as Mami makes her seem. Abuela's love is stern and gently embracing. It holds us in between the French bread she slathers in butter and dips in her café con leche. She is sick but cannot see it yet. She places us in front of the telenovelas. We learn that Spanish women are sultry, and sexy, and dramatic, and loud, and crazy. We learn that life is full of drama and chaos and struggle and pain. We learn that women behave

*like flies caught in the web of men and money. Wriggling in skirts, and
heels, and eye shadow only to further fasten our fate and be devoured by
phallic ruthlessness.*

II. NewYoricana

"¡Mami, mira!" I point at the pigeon on the fire escape of my
grandmother's one-bedroom American dream. Three daughters,
two mothers, one family.

"Berry nice-ee," Mami says without looking out the window.
The screen with the telenovelas hypnotizes her further.

My sister and I hover and ask questions that bother her. We
play too loudly and we run too quickly and we are not welcome
here. America is not like our island of coqui calls and tropical
echoes. Here, we are always inside and quiet, the only green the
philodendron within the hanging basket under my grandmother's
eyes—not like our island where the dirt touched the mud touched
our souls. Instead it is the snow that touches me here in this vast
space full of fluorescent sadness.

At night Mami dresses and heads toward the places that make
her feel like the women in the telenovelas. Our grandmother
watches over us as the city of New York swallows Mami's soul.
Just like the characters she idolizes on the bright neon screen of
possibilities.

*My tongue too fat inside my mouth. Words too slick for my tongue.
My tongue, with its heavy R's and soft Y's. With its sticky papaya P's
and sizzling salami S's. Two islands on my tongue. Two Islands on my
tongue.*

Mami cries all the time now. She yells all the time now. She's sick all the time now. The walls are always white, and the sky is always gray, and the birds always honk, and the parrots always blast their songs of pain and agony in the early morning Bronx bachata. But still she goes out. The men, they holler and they praise but they never stay. A product of '90s disco and New York grime. The white lines on the table hide her face like the bars on our confinement. The iguanas cannot, will not, come inside anymore. I am throwing rocks at them, hoping they'll disappear with my tongue's heavy accent. And soon we move away from Abuelita because Mami cannot stand her Castilian composure.

It was always cold here and it has always been cold to me. Like the cruel lady stepmother who does not want my glass slipper to fit. I pine for the lives on the screen now too. Remembering when mothers were mothers like Mami.

"Hey, spic!"

I look at the boy and am puzzled. His eyes the same color of the water in my soul. Clear and green and blue and seeing me. He is the same toasted coconut of my mother and grandmother and my cousins. Unlike my sister and I who are like Brugal. Mixed and aged and made.

I smile. "My name no Spic. Es—"

Cutting me off, he spits in my face. "You and your dirty sister don't belong on this side of the street." He pushes me into the reality of the gutters. His olive skin the base toxicity of a race we never asked to be a part of. "No spic English, no spic English." He sings and laughs. He laughs and sings. Then starts to skip down toward the store where both our mothers buy oregano, tomatoes, and garlic.

In this city the hurricanes call out to me as they give me their

great flood and wash away the boy in a rage during the gales of
March.

III. Pilgrim

*We live someplace colder now—a place where immigrants landed just
like us. Mami's body begins to wither in the wintry embrace of her ill-
ness. Yet she continues her fairy tale and hides her expiration date. She
flees again, leaving the iguanas to cross the oceans, highways, and certain death for her. Soon, Abuelita is dead. There is no more yelling on
the phone about how hecha y derecha she is. She has no one to explain
her freedoms and liberties to. Gone is the great matriarchal Hope. Es-
peranza is no more. I am no one here except the girl who came from the
place we all came from.*

"You weren't born here?" My classmate's eyes look at me as if I
am some other version of myself. "But your English is . . . *good*. Not
just good, it is *great*." His parents' accent is still heavy on his tongue
even though he was born here and I was not.

In this new place I beam with pride. I no longer possess the
tongue of mar y sol. I am now a real Americana just like the girls
in the lifetime telenovelas who overcome and make it to Harvard.
"That will be me one day," I say. Spring has awakened me.

*We were all on the school bus the first time I was introduced to the
rules of Adam. To the power allowed Lilith but not Eve. Boys gave me
the key to womanhood and I was now an Americana who rolled up her
skirt when she got on the school bus and put on the lip gloss she hid in a
pencil case and shaved her legs without permission.*

"*Chacho, nena, pero que greña.*" The beautician looks at my head
in disgust.

We are sitting in the salon learning that all men lie and cheat and that all women suffer. The rollers on my head smell like acrylic, Tommy Girl, and the humid smoke of hair fighting to maintain its crimp while the heating tools repress it into conformity. Into perfect suburban homes with manicured lawns and two cars in the driveway that come home from real jobs. Just like the girls on Walt's channel and that of five-cent movie theaters. I should wait to put on mascara and shave my legs, but I don't. Instead I idolize a freedom I see in the American girls. I am an American girl with a campesina mother who still speaks like a *spic*. Her tongue heavy with arroz con guandules and the food I hate that she makes. I hate her and how she reminds me of the boy who threw me into the gutter. She brings me shame. I am always angry now. Silenced and obedient but violently and savagely angry. I rebel against the iguanas' warnings. I hate them too.

I flee in the early morning light. A Honda Accord and two boys who know no better. Mothers tried the best they could without the fathers who created these Victor-like creatures. They are hidden in forests of excuses, brought out of hiding with bills made of pitchforks, American streets dressed as prosperity, and the result of mobbish poverty.

I beg Mami to leave him, to choose her children over this man, but her response is that I am not the master of her fate and destiny. And in this light and in that temperature I feel abandoned, although it is I who fled this time. I did not understand the life of a single mother who puts up with men to feed her children. I did not see the bruises underneath the cellulose makeup of her skin, of her body. I am no longer a child, I decide, when the whisper arrives in the breeze and I grab the hand of the first stranger the tumbleweeds drag toward me.

That boy with green hair and blond eyes. Made me scrub my father
so that his skin marbled under me into the cold flesh of paper and ink.
All so I could fit into his pockets and his Bible. So I could stay between
the sheets of privilege and power. I scrubbed as much of my island and
beauty and untame into consent. For survival was all at his mercy and
command. While I was with him no one looked twice unless it was dark.

We pull into a desolate park. The park's bones an echo of a
wealthier cousin in a community not abandoned by fathers.

"You better not bitch out." The boy pulls his penis out.

His friends stand outside, their backs to the car and the smell
of cigarettes and Mary Jane wafting in through the splintered window, stabbing me with insecurity. This boy's ride had seemed like
a sanctuary. Yet now I am trapped. I must follow through or else I
know not where I am or what I am going to do. How could I, a girl
of only sixteen, tell these boys of only sixteen that I was afraid and
cold and alone. When we are all just playing adult. If escape had
meant this truth, then every escape I encounter in life will only be
a thunderstorm.

The indigo–blue textile of back-bending labor and cerulean residue
of bondage and conquest. Immigrant ants. Ancestor copycats. All of us.
Tainos, Yorubas, Mayans, Aztecs. Pagans, Celtics, and Saxons alike.
And all the other ancient places I went to that summer are scarred and
pillaged and colonized by polytheistic deserters.

I lived in this way for many moons and suns, a premature
sapling in an open field. I floated, rustled, trickled over the city
of Boston, and some days I still feel the city pummeling into me
during my dreams. I search in her structure for memories of me.
All that stares back are the empty alleys I desperately try to forget.

I am convinced there is not enough space in my mouth for all these dialects and languages. I spit out accents and osmosis. I am no more the girl from D.R. and P.R. I am now a girl from the U.S. and not the islands on my tongue.

I trek, and trudge, and march through more of the city's crevices, finding crumbs of generosity. And then Mami calls. To shame and guilt and lure me back to her hovel of weakness. No more. No shame, pain, and Cain in, within, me. I will no longer be the article of her scheme. As she pleads on the other end of the line, I simper at her distress. The would-be truths that lay behind my eyes reflect the lies she lets inside: that she is both worthless and invisible.

The man with the car kept me the safest. He did not even pick me up or shake me to see what gifts would be allowed him for the Yule, and yet I still gave him the economy of my soul. This man's garden was two bedrooms wide and a television screen long. And I was on his Insula Canaria in his garden of haram. He kept me a resident, my room above two islands next to more islands under three. I am no longer the honored Ivy League hopeful. Instead I have begun to idolize the women in the screen just as my mother before me.

Strength is in the space between my ears, unmarred by the hand of Adam and untouched by the rape of Eve's metra.

IV. Expirer

Mami was sick when I returned. She progressed back to her beginning. The beginning where she sank down into the sky. Here, the roots come into her and grab her ribs and turn her into a large palm tree. And now

the iguanas speak for her. They climb and lie in her leaves and rustle her
awake when I come home. They whisper to me and now I hear them
calling me home in the winds and crashing waves of Salisbury Beach.

"*¡Todo esto fue tu culpa!*" The phone vibrates from the strength of
my mother's sister's voice, "*¡La mataste!*"

"Here, take this." I hand the phone to my younger sister and
walk outside. Looking up at the night sky, I begin to count the
stars.

"Hey, are you okay?" My uncle, Hebel, sits down beside me.
"She says I killed her." I undulate on the patio swing. "Do you
think that's true?"

Hebel gives a deep sigh and looks up at the sky with me. "Do
you think it's true?" He turns toward me and watches me intently—more than likely making sure I do not fall prey to my anx-
ious retaliations to life.

"I think the soap operas killed Mami." I look at him, and he
stares at me as if I have three heads.

Dailihana E. Alfonseca is a writer of fiction and poetry
that intersects the research of mental health, immigrant
identity, body politics, and capitalist media to make ac-
cessible the traumas of immigration and assimilation.
She is currently attaining her master's in health human-
ities at the University of North Carolina–Chapel Hill and
is working on her follow-up short story, "Bachatas Murdered My Father," which touches on how music influ-
ences livability.

Editor's Note

"Schism in a Soul So Tender" is a coming-of-age story where a young woman is isolated while her family seeks out and captures her doppelgänger, implied to have appeared after her sexual awakening. Viewed through the lens of a no-nonsense protagonist, the piece's grounded voice and lyrical prose elevate the mundane moments of fading adolescence. At its heart, the world that Clara Mundy has crafted is dichotomous; women are to be coddled and, simultaneously, expected to cut down every part of themselves that does not fit societal standards of femininity. "Schism in a Soul So Tender" is an intimate exploration of the all-consuming societal pressures, especially sexual, that women face and what exactly is lost in trying to become the version of yourself the world wishes to see. Mundy elegantly weaves a world that seems removed in place and time from our own but resonates deeply with modern experiences of womanhood.

We were instantly grabbed by the concept of the piece—mysterious, eldritch circumstances that have left a young woman practically bedbound—and the way in which Mundy quietly answers readers' questions through the charming and often pithy voice of the woman herself. The dialogue and scene setting all reveal a world set decades behind our own, but the construct of doppelgängers and the ever-relevant thematic commentary lend the piece a timeless quality.

Emily Lin, Literary Editor
Apricity Magazine

Schism in a Soul So Tender

Clara Mundy

I LIVE IN A MANY-PEOPLED CABIN. THEY WILL NOT let me work or clean, nor help tend the animals. They will not let me run. On the days I rise from bed, I go downstairs and try to at least help with the dishes. But whoever is there, usually Aunt Terry, will not hear of it. She shoos me away, nudging me by my elbows back up the stairs and between the stale sheets.

Only women live in the cabin, for the time being. My aunt and cousin move in and out of the house; there are four of us in total. I envy their mobility, particularly that of my cousin Alice. She is only nine, with curls like coiled ribbon. She tends to the cows, giving them hay and ensuring they return to the correct field every night. It was my job, once, and I was wonderful at it. I could walk side by side with the animals, knowing they would not kick or charge or resent my presence. It is a skill none of the others have. Even Alice, calm as she is around the cattle, dares not go within a few feet of them.

This morning I tried to make myself useful. I all but begged Aunt Terry to give me a chore, a task, anything to fill the hours, but she recycled her dissents and forced me back to my room. Not my actual room, mind, just the room I'm staying in for now. I've spent hours staring at the ceiling, memorizing its cracks and scuffs, its upside-down topography.

There's a knock on the door, after which it immediately opens.

SCHISM IN A SOUL SO TENDER

No time to get up. Mother walks in, her face tired but her hair freshly washed, one hand behind her back. She sits on the edge of the bed, running her hands along the faded quilt.

"Terry says you went downstairs again," she says.

"I only wanted to help," I say.

"You know you shouldn't." She smiles at me, tucks a hair behind my ear. "Here, I was going through some boxes and found more of Nanna's old books. I don't think you've read these."

She pulls out her hidden hand and places three volumes in my lap. They're leather bound, titles unfamiliar. I flip through them. Time has faded the pages, rendering them nearly illegible. The books range from two hundred to five hundred pages, enough to keep me busy for at least three days.

We've had no visitors to distract us from my situation. A landline stands guard in the kitchen, but it's been mostly silent since my bed rest began. My friends called the first few days, hoping to arrange shopping trips and visits to the city. But my mother and aunt told them what had happened, why I wouldn't be at school for the following weeks. My friends who had gone through it themselves—Ashley and Tabitha, both a year older than me—sent assurances that I would be just fine. My other friend, Bailey, the baby of our group who had yet to experience the same, simply apologized and hung up. I hoped Tom Maurice would call, but if his voice crackled through our receiver, they never told me of it.

ALICE COMES IN later. She carries a chipped white bowl filled with oranges, which she sets on my nightstand. She stands by the bed for a moment, eyeing the books and sneaking glances at me.

Some days I invite her to join me; we lie together and eat fruit and imagine ourselves worlds away. But this afternoon, I see the perspiration on her temples from running outside with the cows, and my stomach contracts. I thank her; she drags her feet as she walks out.

I peel the oranges, savoring the feel of their rind beneath my fingernails. The juices spilling down my hands are heaven—everything in this room, the sheets and the books and the wood furniture, is dry and stagnant. When I leave it, there will be no indication of the months it sheltered me. These oranges grew until my aunt or cousin or mother plucked them from the tree. They reveal layers, peel giving way to wrinkled slices giving way to stem. The slices cling to each other as I pull them apart, begging not to be separated from their brood. I swallow their liquid sunlight, pretending it's enough to ease my withdrawals. Once I've eaten a few pieces, I look into the orange, the stem and wedges remaining, and there I see myself. It's been happening a lot, recently. There are no mirrors in the room, so I rely on the fruit to reflect my image. It never disappoints. I am always there, in the curve between slice and stem, in the peach pit and the apple seeds buried within the flesh. It comforts me to discover my likeness in fruit, plentiful and resilient. But I cannot help thinking of all those who eat me, and how even I eat me, and I wonder if the continuous death is worth the never-ending life.

I wipe my hands of these musings and resume eating. I lie on my side, allowing some juice to spill from my lips and onto the white sheets.

———

AUNT TERRY COMES in a few hours later to collect the bowl. She scowls at the slightly orange, sticky stains from where the juice spilled.

"Up, up," she says. She strips the sheets from the bed, bundling them under her arm. She looks around the room, at the empty mattress and the single wooden chair hiding in the corner. "Well, I guess you'll come downstairs while I clean these."

I do not smile, worried that a sign of my happiness will result in its confiscation. I follow her down the steps, lifting my nightdress to prevent tripping. The material fills my hand with its thickness, its texture grates against my palms—a relic from my grandmother's sewing days. She died many years ago, but Mother ensured her clothes were well-preserved. I've worn it for five days, maybe six.

Though I'm downstairs, Aunt Terry will not let me work. The grumbling of the washing machine makes the floors vibrate. I sit on the couch, listening to her prepare dinner, inspecting the painting which hangs above the fireplace. It depicts the cabin, set against a wistful sky and surrounded by grass. A horse tied to the porch stares out of the painting and at me.

Alice squeals; soft *thumps* announce her jumping on the porch. She runs through the door, grabbing her mother's dress. "Someone's coming!"

"What?" Aunt Terry asks, abandoning the kitchen, following her outside. Alice sees me, does a double take, looks at her mother in confusion.

"I'm washing her sheets," Aunt Terry explains, pushing her daughter out the door with her. "Can you tell who it is?"

"Not yet, but it's not the truck," The door closes behind them but still I listen. Mother's voice mingles with theirs.

"Looks like Rich's car to me," she says. Her eyesight is better than all of ours. She always says I could have been the same if only I ate more carrots as a child.

"You're right," Terry says.

"Daddy!" Alice shouts, followed by a few claps of her hands. The roar of wheels against gravel grows louder, then stops.

"Who do we have here?" Uncle Rich says.

"Any news?" Mother asks.

"'Course," he says. "But can't a man get something to eat? Been driving since this morning."

They hurry him in, no one casting a glance at me in the living room. Alice holds one of his massive hands in both of hers, Terry wipes at the dust on his face, Mother takes off his coat. They grab at him as if hoping that touch alone could impart the knowledge he has to share.

Terry and Mother go to the kitchen. Rich lifts Alice in the air, spins her around until she squeals. He stops when he notices me.

"Well, look who it is," he says, words booming through the small room. Mother jokes that her brother-in-law has no concept of an inside voice.

Besides the general uncleanliness, he looks the same as I remember—portly, tall enough to reach the ceiling, a mole underneath his left eye, eyes that soften his whole appearance and make one glad to be around him.

"Food's ready," Mother says.

Alice runs to the kitchen, the squeak of table legs against the floor emphasizing her eagerness. Rich extends a hand toward me.

"You'll join us?" he asks.

Mother wants to object, I see the words stringing together in her mind, but I take his hand and follow. Terry also tries to say something when I sit down, but Rich puts his hand up, the closest he can get to an order.

"She deserves to know," he says. "Besides, it's for her sake all this is happening."

Terry acquiesces, sits beside her daughter and across from her husband. Mother joins us, and we pick at the ham-and-mustard sandwiches while Rich swallows them in a few bites.

"We found it yesterday," he says, sticking a thumb under his waistband. "Hiding out in one of those no-name towns, working in a bar."

"Oh, god," says Terry. Her eyes flick to me, sympathizing with my misfortune.

"What's it calling itself?" Mother asks.

Rich looks at the table. "Susan."

Terry moans; Alice's eyes widen at her distress. Mother's hand tightens around her cup, her eyes turning to flint.

"It's bold, I'll give it that," she says. "Taking my girl's face, and her name too."

"You remember how it is," Rich says. He tries smiling at his daughter to alleviate her worries, but Alice is staring at Terry, whose head is buried in her hands. "It'll do whatever it can to get by, don't matter what kinda morality it's breaking. We'll take care of it now the same as then."

Mother nods. "You'll go straight to bed after this," she says to me. "Gotta preserve your energy." Turning to Rich, she asks when my father will arrive.

"Tomorrow morning, most like," he replies. "It was easy enough to subdue the thing, but it kept trying to act up when it was awake.

We used some a' Terry's pills to keep it asleep, so hopefully, that'll speed him up."

"Tomorrow, then," Mother says. She reaches across the table, pats my hand. "You hear that, baby? It's almost over."

I chew and chew and chew on the sandwich until it turns to mush in my mouth, until it's all I can focus on, until I wonder if I'll choke on it, then I swallow.

I SLEEP ON the sheets Terry washed. When I wake up, I feel cold. I will be allowed to walk today, to go outside and breathe fresh air. I want to lose myself in the sensation of stretched legs, exertion, running for the sake of it. But there's a buzzing in my ears, not loud enough for a headache, nor quiet enough to be ignored.

A knock on the door, Mother walks in. A folded white dress rests in her arms.

"How do you feel?" she asks.

I shrug.

She lays the dress on the chair, sits in front of me on the bed. "Listen, I know it's scary. But remember, this happened to me, it happened to your Aunt Terry, every woman has to go through it. You're not alone."

"Do I have to be the one to do it?" I ask. "Dad can't? Rich?"

Mother shakes her head. "We tried that for Terry. She couldn't bear the thought of doing it. Your granddad did it instead, and a month later, a new one popped up. It was stronger than the first and put up quite the fight, but that time we insisted Terry be the one. She didn't like it, of course, but there was never a third. I'm sorry sweetheart, but it can't be anyone else."

"What was it like for you?" I ask.

"Mine was tough," she admits. "It tried everything it could to survive: begging, crying, screaming. It had all my memories, and it used 'em against me to get me to waver. But I didn't."

"What if I waver?"

Mother cups my chin as when I was a child. "We'll all be beside you. It's your hand that has to do it, but that doesn't mean we can't help."

"And then I won't have to stay in here all day?"

Mother smiles. "No, no. Staying in the room was my father's idea during Terry's second time. He thought the restlessness would help make the thing's protests less effective. Today's the last day you'll have to spend here, I promise."

I nod, thinking of the cows and the peace of standing among them, of feeling their massive bodies graze mine and knowing I was protected.

I HEAR MY father's truck an hour later. It roars, scaring the cows and Alice. Even my arm hairs rise a bit. I am still in my room, sitting on the bed, the white dress replacing my nightgown. It's an old garment, thick and long-sleeved, more suitable for the winter than our current summer day. It's a size too small, causing my skin to billow where the neckline and sleeves end. The dress is not necessary for the day's proceedings but another touch of my grandfather's—he was a theatrical man and embraced the ritualistic possibilities of this moment.

Someone knocks on my door, but they do not enter. When I open it, my mother stands before me. She takes my hand and leads me downstairs, where Terry holds on to Alice. My cousin cannot stop moving. She taps her feet, scratches her arms, looks at me and then the floor. They are both in cream dresses, similar to my mother's, inappropriate for summer. Sweat accumulates at my aunt's hairline, which she smudges away.

Mother's grip on me is tight. I use her arm like a column for support.

"Where is it?" I ask.

"Tied up outside," she says. "The boys are getting ready."

A moment later they join us in their own cream shifts, less adorned than the women's. My father's face is worn, dirty. I have not seen him in two months, not since it appeared and he began hunting. I hope he will hug me, but he only glances in my direction and says it's time.

We walk into the midday heat, to the post on the side of the house where I would tie the horse I had as a child. The horse died three years ago, heart bursting as I rode. Now, hands tied against the post, head lolling, my reflection stands.

The double is exactly that—same hair, same skin tone, every detail a perfect replica. I have not seen it since it first appeared, the same day Tom Maurice and I walked along the creek. He kissed me and I was so surprised, so delighted, I let him touch me wherever he wanted. The realization of my own desirability made me drunk. I slipped into the creek more than once and my shoes were still wet as I returned to our fields, imagining what I'd tell my friends the next morning. When I finished giving the cows hay, I turned around and it was there, naked and shaking, clutching at my ankles as it begged for help. But Mother had warned me—story after story of them stealing husbands, sleeping with other men only for the original woman to carry the child. So I kicked it and ran to the house, screaming for my parents. By the time I found them, told them, led them to the spot, it was gone. And so, the search began.

Today, the double is not naked. It wears a tattered dress, straps barely hanging on to the shoulders, chest exposed. Cuts and bruises adorn its face and body, likely my father's doing. Its eyelids are purple, swollen, but they lift so that the double sees me.

Its features are stoic before noticing my family behind me, the knife that my mother presses into my hands. Unlike our clothes, the weapon is not ceremonial—it's from the kitchen and afterward will be used to prepare dinner.

Eyes flick from knife to me, family to knife to me. It shakes its head, pushes against the stake as if to merge with it.

"Please, Susan," it says, voice no different from my own.

I watch the double struggle against the rope, expecting its form to break, its otherness to be revealed. But it remains in one body, a body no stronger than my own.

A hand pushes against my back, Mother's or Father's. I move a few steps closer, wondering how to hold the knife. I have only ever used it for cutting fruit, vegetables—nothing that would resent the violence.

"You don't have to," it says, lips trembling.

Why didn't Father gag her? Is this part of the tradition as well? That I listen to my own self die to live again?

It looks so much like me that I cannot register the resemblance. The moment feels like finding a picture of myself from when I was

little, one I've never seen before, noticing my familiar features con-
torted in unfamiliar ways.

I raise the knife, preparing myself to plunge it once and deep
and have it over with.

"Wait!" it screeches. "Just let me tell you one thing, one secret."

I feel my family's attention on me like a wet coat. My family,
who has moved freely through the world while I've been locked up
for months. My family, who promises this will be over but whom
I can't absolutely believe. To listen to the double is to prolong my
assured freedom. So I step forward, close enough for it to whisper.

Its breath is warm and shaky against my neck. The scent of it
fills my nose, my own but mixed with blood and intensified by our
joint presence.

"What you did, it wasn't bad," the double whispers. "Don't let
them tell you otherwise."

I hear footsteps behind me, my father's. I am sure he has grown
impatient. I do not allow myself to think, to listen to the words it
continues to say. I force the knife into the double's chest, pulling
in and out and in and out, encountering less resistance each time.
It whimpers, words abandoned. I look over its shoulder at the cows
as it convulses, as it coughs blood into my hair, as its empty head
falls onto my shoulder.

EVERYONE IS TOO busy preparing dinner to help me wash out
the blood. Rich at least runs a bath, making it warm to calm my
supposedly fragile nerves. He leaves to help my father prepare the
meat.

I scrub myself raw, dragging the washcloth against my face

even after the blood is gone. I have an urge to take off all my layers, the clothes and the skin and the muscle and the bone. I want to be only essence, as it now is.

MOTHER AND AUNT Terry cook a feast that night. I smell it from my room, my real room with the blue curtains and flowered quilt and paintings of imaginary lives. I've been allowed back in, now that I'm clean and the danger is gone. I run my hands over the trinkets—music boxes, old jewelry, favorite books. Despite my months of rest, I want to crawl into my bed, disguise myself in the sheets, like a letter in an envelope. But I hear the clashes of pans give way to small talk, signaling that it's time to eat.

The chatter ceases when I walk downstairs. Mother and Aunt Terry and Uncle Rich smile, Alice looks at me with wider eyes than usual. Father folds my body into a hug, lifting me off the ground as when I was little.

"It's so good to see you," he whispers into my hair. "I've missed you so much, Susan, so much."

I return his hug, though absently. My attention falls toward the table, where every platter we own is arranged and overflowing with food. There's the salad, the potatoes, the corn and other sides, but more than anything there is the meat. It flows like a river through the table, every other dish covered in what was once me.

We sit, we eat, Father serving me as the guest of honor.

"Let us be glad," he says, his voice booming. "Our Susan has looked into the face of evil, and she has vanquished it. It's thanks to her that we are all together again."

The other adults nod. Alice looks at me. She has not stopped looking at me since I came down. I recognize in her still manner and raised skin the realization that I had when my mother told me about her double. *It'll be me next. It'll be her next.*

My jaw moves in methodical circles as I chew. I think it's meat in my mouth, but I can't be sure—my attention keeps going out of focus. I look at the platters and see it, her, for now, I can see that she couldn't have just been an *it*. If she were, she would have disappeared, floated into the wind the minute I killed her. But she was real and substantive, she had a body that I killed and Father took apart and Mother cooked to a tender medium-rare. A body that I chew, that we all chew.

"I hear Tom Maurice has been thinking of settling down," Aunt Terry says. She speaks around the food in her mouth, covering it with her hand in mock courtesy. Beside her, Uncle Rich shovels forkful after forkful into himself, hardly looking up.

"You and he always got along, right, Susan?" Mother asks.

I nod, my mouth full of her, having the decency to not let my future mix with her death. The memories of the creek do not bring the same excitement as before.

Mother sees my nod and shoots a glance first at my father, then Terry. They all smile and raise their eyebrows.

"Not hungry, Su?" Rich asks. He's bent over his plate, a bit of juice leaking out of the corner of his lips.

I've had only a few bites, but I know that any more would make my body cave in on itself. I shake my head, look down.

"It's been a long day," Father says, laying a hand on mine. "You'll have a better appetite tomorrow. Your aunt and mother will wrap up some of the leftovers, no trouble."

I offer a grateful smile. Tomorrow my appetite will also be

poor, and the next day and the next, until the meat spoils and no one can eat it.

"Oh, your friend Bailey, her mother called today," Aunt Terry says. "Seems her time has come too. I doubt you'll be able to speak with her, but you could call and leave a message of support with her parents. It helped us when your friends did the same."

I mumble okay, thinking of Bailey with her pink bows, laughter that blended so well with mine. I remember Tabitha and Ashley hoping she would be spared.

"If you're up to it," Father says, "why don't you go bring in the cows? I'm sure they've missed you."

His words dissipate the fog, bringing the room back into focus. "Really?" I ask.

He nods, I look at Mother, she nods, I get up. The scraping of utensils against plates continues as I leave the cabin and walk across the yard. The cows have been grazing in the larger pasture all day, fattening themselves. They're well-trained and docile and begin walking toward the barn once I open the gate that separates them. When I've watched, Alice has retreated at this point, sitting on the edge of the fence as they make their way inside. I stand in the middle of the gate, waiting for the cows to approach. And they do—calmly, slowly, as if they had not noticed my absence the past two months. First, there are only a few, then the rest follow, crowding together and parting around me like a river makes way for a stone.

When we are so close that I can feel how each of their textures differs, one of the calves tries to gnaw my hand. I flinch as its teeth graze my skin; it moves on, unaffected. My heart constricts. My resolve folds into itself, opening the door for fear—that the cows will stampede, that I'll be trampled underneath them, that they'll push me far into the earth, deeper than where the double came from, and no one will be able to find me. I hold my elbows, make myself smaller, but they only get closer. The cows don't look at me—they rarely do, but the absence of their gaze never made me feel less close to them until now. Even as I search for the peace they once inspired, the euphoria that I could only attain in their presence, I know it is futile. By the time the last cow passes me, I am crouching on the ground, heaves making my chest swell and contract to such a degree that I feel I'll burst open. The lack of connection stings as severely as a missing limb, as if it too was stabbed and dismantled and eaten by us all.

Clara Mundy studied English, French, and creative writing at the University of Texas at Austin. Originally from a Texas cattle ranch, she has gathered inspiration for her stories from both her rural upbringing and her time spent gallivanting around Europe. Her short story "Schism in a Soul So Tender" received the 2021 Roy Crane Award for Outstanding Achievement in the Literary Arts.

Editors' Note

"Filth" by Verity McKay is a masterful microflash piece. The writing is crisp and evocative, the emotions are raw, and the revelations are shocking. McKay fixes her gaze on a sharp moment in time and presents it to her audience in excruciating detail. "Filth" contains no context, yet simultaneously provides every bit of context. There's a perfect balance between what is revealed and what is withheld. We knew instantly it belonged in *Hypertext* and we were beyond honored to give it a home.

Chelsea Laine Wells, Fiction and Managing Editor
Bryan Lindsey, Contributing Editor
Hypertext Magazine

Filth

Verity McKay

ONE EVENING, MY WIFE SHED HER RUBBER GLOVES
and decided she'd had enough. "I can't pretend anymore," she said.
"I won't."

I pitied her. She wasn't a natural housewife. Black armbands,
formed of oven grease, encircled her elbows. Guiding her to the
sink, I rinsed away the grimy oases pooling in the folds of her skin.

"You rest. I'll put the kettle on," I said. I led her to the table and
sat her down. "Don't stress. I bet your mum'll be willing to lend a
hand."

"It was my fault."

I placed her mug down on the counter and turned. She faced
a photo hanging on the wall: the one with the layer of dust atop
its gilded frame—a blight on our otherwise spotless home, best
ignored. Jamie. Her face a shriveled peach; her planet-sized eyes
glittering with unfulfilled mischief. We'd agreed she couldn't be
replaced. We'd never make another like her.

"What do you mean?" I said.

I waited. The kettle rumbled, like the onset of a distant tsunami.

"She was blue when I reached the cot," she said. "It may have
been too late by then, but I didn't check. I pretended I hadn't seen.
I left her there for ten minutes before I called the ambulance."

She squeezed her palms together, her eyes brimming. Behind

her, a spider tightroped across a cobweb spanning the length of the curtain rail. Funny how a man can see the same four corners every day and not notice the intricate details of the space he inhabits.

"You were never there," she said. "Everything rested on me—it was too much."

I crossed the room and reached for the paperweight from the end table. Jamie—frozen, immaculate—watched me through her neglected frame. I stared at the center of my wife's crown—at the same point where the soft spot on our daughter's skull would never fuse—and raised the paperweight above my head.

She went rigid, like prey, and closed her eyes.

The kettle clicked. I lowered my shaking arm, and turned my back on both of them.

Verity McKay is a teacher by day and a fiction writer by night. She likes animals, kickboxing, and reading as many books as she can get her hands on. She is currently working on her short story collection, *In Between Worlds*, which explores the physical and psychological states of transition that we are all subject to on our journeys through life.

Editor's Note

Mengyin Lin was one of *Epiphany*'s 2022 Breakout Prize winners in prose. Her story "Magic, or Something Less Assuring" was chosen by our guest judge for the contest that year, Nadia Owusu. I was lucky enough to work with Mengyin in an editorial capacity.

The story is deceptively straightforward: a couple from Shanghai take one last trip together, to Morocco, during the mandatory "cooling-off period" between filing for and finalizing their divorce. Though its events unfold over just a few days, the heavily expository third-person narrative voice, which moves gracefully between the two protagonists' perspectives, allows the reader a rich and nuanced understanding of their history: their years of love, their differences and complications, and all that's led to this last, melancholy moment.

It is a beautifully written piece, which feels at once timeless and utterly of its time. In a key scene, the divorcing couple is asked by a young medical student about the stringent quarantine protocols that initially limited the spread of COVID-19 in China but led to other deaths—for instance, as the wife points out, "a paralyzed boy whose caretaker was sent to mandatory quarantine." In their snappish, well-worn argument, the pair embody the essential tension of that recent moment in our political history, yet they remain compelling, dimensional characters.

Yet even as the story does justice to their humanity, it contextualizes the ephemerality of their disagreement—and of them. In the story's virtuosic yet understated final paragraph, they watch the sun go down on the Sahara, dwarfed by the grandeur of their surroundings. The temporal boundaries of the story are transcended, and the reader is given, as in our best literature, a brief glimpse of their—and our own—ultimate insignificance.

Rachel Lyon, Former Editor in Chief
Epiphany

Magic, or Something Less Assuring

Mengyin Lin

"MAYBE WE SHOULDN'T KISS IN PUBLIC HERE," SAID the woman.

"Yeah? Yeah. Though I heard this is one of the more open countries," said the man.

Waiting in line to get through customs at Tangier Ibn Battouta Airport, Ting and Si-Bo couldn't help but overhear the conversation between the young couple in front of them. Ting had seen them on the airport bus in Madrid, kissing then, too. It seemed that, surrounded by Moroccan policemen in the arrival hall, they were finally realizing that they had arrived in a place where it was indecent to put romantic affection on public display. The crown of the woman reached to the stubbled chin of the man, a perfect height difference for her to nestle her head against his shoulder. Ting wondered if they were on their honeymoon. When she did her research for this trip, she thought Morocco would make an interesting honeymoon destination for couples who were looking for more than a torch-lit dinner on the beach and rose petals afloat in a warm bath. That kind of formulaic, frivolous staging of romance had never charmed Ting. The performative aspect of it made her uncomfortable. Her fondest memories of her relationship with Si-Bo consisted of no materialistic attributes: they were quiet, fleeting moments when it felt as if they were the only lovers alive.

The line was barely moving. Ting craned her neck to get a look at the customs booths. Out of the row of a dozen windows, only three were functioning with immigration officers behind. It was impossible not to look at the couple less than a meter in front of her. They had retreated to looking at each other now, the woman's head tilting up and the guy's neck bending toward her face. Ting recognized the look in their eyes. They were in love, as she and Si-Bo had once been. Only people who have been in love can recognize other people in love, Ting thought. It was like an exclusive tribe, the moment of "I see you." One was either in or out. As if she'd felt Ting's gaze, the woman turned to look at Ting. Ting smiled and the woman, noticing Si-Bo next to her, returned a knowing grin. Ting was happy to see other people in love, even though she had to suppress her fatalistic belief that every couple would fall out of love eventually, temporarily or permanently.

Ting and Si-Bo had never gone on a honeymoon when they married four years ago, and neither of them could remember why. They had been together for eleven years and many things had happened without logic or reason. Ting couldn't quite put her finger on when their relationship shifted into autopilot. It had always been Ting and Si-Bo, Si-Bo and Ting, as if nothing had existed before or would change in the future. They both accepted this stasis. Eleven years was a whole lifetime when they were only thirty years old. The eternity they had spent being each other's other half had rendered it alien, inconceivable to imagine otherwise. Ting didn't see Si-Bo as a separate individual but as an extension of herself. And Si-Bo didn't know who Ting was but first his girlfriend, then his wife. Even after they had walked out of the marriage bureau on a gloomy October afternoon two weeks ago, each holding a copy of

their divorce application form, Si-Bo held Ting's bag, as he had always done, because Ting had bad shoulders from sitting at her desk
for long periods, and Ting reached for and pulled out the collar of
Si-Bo's peacoat, which he often left carelessly folded inward. Both
of them admitted only retroactively that they had been, perhaps
intentionally, overlooking the seismic reshaping and reshuffling
of the psychological blocks that made them who they were, like
humans who remain ignorant of the movement of tectonic plates
until an earthquake demolishes civilizations and buries lives. That
afternoon, they called for separate cars to take them away from
their marriage. They had already confessed to their parents, who
called them fools; she had already moved out of the apartment that
was registered in his name. Si-Bo's car arrived first. Ting watched
it shrink smaller and smaller on the Shanghai street. She had only
known this city as Si-Bo's wife. When his car disappeared around
the corner, she greeted the trees, buildings, cars, and pedestrians of
Shanghai as a new person, as Ting without Si-Bo.

Ting couldn't have known that Si-Bo was doing the same, his
eyes on her in the side-view mirror as she shrank into a tiny black
dot he was unable to differentiate from the other black dots on the
sidewalk. Si-Bo thought that was the last time he was going to see
Ting for a while. The next would be some time after thirty days,
the legally required "cooling-off period," when they would go back
to the marriage bureau to finalize their divorce. He assumed that
he would not be coming on the Morocco trip, which happened to
fall during this mandatory grace period. Ting had booked the trip
for them almost a year ago, as soon as the government loosened the
draconian quarantine measures for international traveling. Si-Bo
understood that the invitation to travel with his wife, along with

their marriage, was no longer valid—and Ting was still his wife, until their photos were pasted, and their names printed, on identical divorce certificates.

He figured Ting would go on her own, regardless. She had wanted to go to Morocco for so long. She had bought nonrefundable, nontransferrable plane tickets at the lowest prices, paid for accommodations in advance at a discounted rate, and booked the most cost-efficient tour guides to go into the Sahara. Frugality was one of her principles. She never pursued luxury. But that was only part of why she'd planned the trip the way she did: more importantly, she hadn't wanted to leave open any possibility of change. When she set her mind on something, she made sure it would happen. Their divorce was not going to change her mind. That much he still knew about Ting, he thought with confidence, though he couldn't forget the way the muscles around her right eye twitched as she'd called him a stranger, over and over, in the multitude of fights that had chipped away at their union.

So when he showed up at the airport check-in line next to Ting, and told her that he hadn't been sure if he would see her there, they both knew well that it was a big fat lie. Of course if Ting had asked him to leave, he would have, but she didn't. Since the day at the marriage bureau, he had not heard from her. They hadn't had a reason to be in touch. It had surprised Si-Bo, once they stopped living under the same roof and carrying out their filial duty as a couple, how thoroughly their lives had operated in separate universes. Now, here they were, in this foreign airport, where the incomprehensible Arabic script unnerved him, knowing not a soul but each other. Perhaps one last trip as a married couple would make up for the fact that they hadn't had a honeymoon. Perhaps this trip would draw a clean ending for the eleven years they'd loved each other. Perhaps, just perhaps, by the slightest chance, this foreign land would rain fairy dust upon them and turn them into the couple standing before them, who had just resumed kissing.

"Do you think couples should go on one last trip together before they get divorced?" Si-Bo whispered into Ting's ear in Mandarin, making sure other Chinese tourists couldn't hear him.

Ting took a step forward in the moving line as she pondered the question. When Si-Bo caught up, she said, "Like a divorce honeymoon?"

They shared a laugh. Ting didn't hate Si-Bo. In the man standing next to her she still recognized the shadows of the boy she loved. She couldn't withdraw the love she had deposited ceaselessly for eleven years all at once even if she tried—and she had tried. She was only repulsed by how he thought about the world, which was in every way different from how she did. Were his thoughts and his person the same thing? She wasn't sure. She herself often had thoughts that shocked her. If she thought about stabbing someone when a knife was in sight, did that make her a murderer? If she thought about getting hit by a car when crossing the street, or jumping onto the tracks when the subway rumbled into the station, was she suicidal? No, Ting argued with herself, as she often spent hours doing. Those were transient, unpredictable thoughts, while Si-Bo's despicable views were sustained and fully formed. What defined a person if not these inventions of the mind? Ting could go on and on like this, throwing these questions up in the air and letting them linger, hovering above her like dark clouds before a storm. One day, when the clouds gathered enough substance to produce a deluge, she'd let it all fall. It was when she was soaked with exhaustion, confusion, and all the other emotions that she couldn't individually name, which had been brewing in those clouds, that she surrendered her intellect, closed her eyes, and— against her instinct—felt. It became clear to her then. There had been only one question all along: Did she still want to spend the rest of her life with Si-Bo? No. She didn't.

The couple in front of them left the line. A moment later, it was Ting and Si-Bo's turn. They walked up to an officer's window and handed over their passports.

"Where are you from in China?" the customs officer asked, without looking up from his desk.

"Shanghai," said Si-Bo.

"Xi'An," said Ting. Hearing Si-Bo, she added, "But I live in Shanghai."

"What do you do?"

"I work in finance," replied Si-Bo.

"I'm a translator," replied Ting.

"For what?" The customs officer glanced at Ting with interest.

"Books, mostly. And news articles, art catalogs, anything I can get, basically. I freelance."

The officer wasn't really listening. He was typing on his computer and scribbling words on papers, glancing back and forth between the two of them. He was silent for an oddly long period and Ting started to get nervous. Many years of going through U.S. customs had made this a nerve-wracking occasion for no reason. The customs officer flipped their passports to the photo page. He looked intently at Ting and Si-Bo, as if he were trying to memorize the outlines of their features. In his pupils, Ting saw the reflection of Si-Bo and herself, standing side by side in the same way they had for their portrait on the marriage certificate, and felt obliged to provide a verbal footnote.

"We're divorced," Ting volunteered.

Si-Bo raised his eyebrows in protest. "No, we're not."

Si-Bo had turned to look at Ting but Ting kept her head straight. The smile she had put on her face was fighting to keep its shape.

"Well, yeah, not officially," Ting said.

"Not officially," Si-Bo emphasized.

The customs officer gave them a baffled look as he stamped their passports, one after the other, and pushed them out under the windowpane. "Welcome to Morocco."

THEIR GUESTHOUSE SENT a driver to pick them up. Seeing Ting pointing at the frail piece of paper in his hand, he pushed himself off the column he'd been leaning against and took Ting's luggage without a smile. Ting wondered if he was upset about their late arrival. She was oversensitive to other people's emotions and habitually blamed herself for their unhappiness.

"Do you think he's mad at us or something?" Ting asked Si-Bo as they trailed the driver in the airport parking lot.

As soon as the question left Ting's lips, she wished she could take it back. She knew all too well that it was not going to be a matter of concern for Si-Bo, who, in situations where Ting incriminated herself, always absolved himself, instinctively and effortlessly, of any responsibility. If he didn't think he'd done anything wrong, he wouldn't care how his actions affected anyone else. Si-Bo attributed this dissonance between them to the difference between male and female sensibilities, as though these were innate, universal traits of all men and women. Ting had told him that their differences were not between men and women, but between traditional masculinity and femininity, which were social rather than biological constructs. But men and women do have indisputable biological differences, Si-Bo would say, and Ting would struggle to find an effective line of reasoning to dispute it. She knew that Si-Bo had eventually stopped arguing with her to appease her, and she had refuted his argument enough times that she promised herself that she would not expend her energy on it any longer. What Si-Bo thought was none of her business anymore. It was no longer her business to change him. Still, she wished she could expel the emotionally draining self-criticism that was programmed into her, that never failed to rise up and seize her whenever it could. To change that, in herself, would be enough.

"It's part of the job to wait, isn't it?" Si-Bo answered halfheartedly. He had other things on his mind. "Why did you have to tell the customs person that we're divorced? He didn't even ask."

"Because we *are* getting a divorce."

"Legally we're still married."

"Is that why you came on this trip with me? To remind me that we're still, *legally*, married?"

"That's not what I meant."

"What did you mean, then?"

The driver arranged their two suitcases in the back of the passenger van and opened the doors to the back seat. Without waiting for an answer from Si-Bo, Ting climbed into the van. After Si-Bo followed inside and the door slid closed automatically, the quiet, liminal interior of a car, with an unsmiling, middle-aged

Moroccan man sitting at the steering wheel, suddenly seemed an inappropriate space in which to continue their disagreement. Si-Bo didn't have an answer anyway. When Ting had proposed the divorce, she'd said they were fundamentally different people. But his parents were different people, her parents were different people—wasn't marriage about loving each other despite their differences? Ting had said "I hate you" many times, but never "I don't love you anymore." There was, Si-Bo believed, a distinction between the two phrases. Love and hate weren't mutually exclusive: one could hate and love another person at the same time. At any rate they were both factually right, and Si-Bo wasn't about to admit to Ting the last bit of hope he had hidden in the corner of his heart.

THE DRIVER DIDN'T speak much English, so Ting couldn't make any progress on figuring out whether he was indeed upset. She appreciated the silent ride into the city instead. The drizzle that Ting and Si-Bo had landed in was phasing into a forceful rain. She watched the falling water soften the edges of the architecture, turning the city into an impressionist painting. As their car wound down to the coastal boulevard, the ancient Medina of Tangier came into view, rising above the Atlantic Ocean on a hill. A jolt of excitement churned in her stomach. It wasn't just that it was her first time out of China since the pandemic but that she was in Morocco. Morocco! Ting felt as if she were in a waking dream.

Ting's obsession with Morocco had started with Sanmao's essay collection *Stories of the Sahara*. The library at her high school in Xi'An had only one copy and it had lost its cover by the time Ting got a hold of it. She was sixteen when she read it, and, like every sixteen-year-old girl who read Sanmao, she instantly wanted to be her. Sanmao loved and suffered with a kind of intensity that didn't seem to exist in the world Ting came from, where adults were trapped in the cycle of clockwork mundanity and insatiable desire to do more, make more, be more. Sanmao was bohemian, worldly, deadly romantic, self-consciously confident. Ting thought if she wasn't going to *be* Sanmao, she was, at least, going to walk on the same sand that the wandering writer had loved.

Si-Bo had agreed to the trip to Morocco without knowing of Ting's childhood admiration for Sanmao. When he thought of Morocco he thought of the first movie they had seen together in New York. Si-Bo had long forgotten the name of the movie. Ting always picked the movies they saw; Si-Bo merely tagged along. This movie starred a pair of vampire lovers and was directed by one of her favorite filmmakers, whose name he also didn't recall. What he did remember was that they watched it on a bright day and the whole movie happened during nighttime, which made him feel as if they were turning into nocturnal animals themselves. When they came out of the theater, he thought he was going to evaporate into black smoke under the sun. Ting loved the movie and told him that the last part of it, wherein the vampire lovers traversed the long and narrow alleys of an ancient town, had been filmed in Tangier. Si-Bo hadn't known where Tangier was until three years ago, when Morocco changed its visa policy for Chinese citizens and Ting started talking about traveling there. Since that movie, he would occasionally end up on those cobbled backstreets in his dreams, where the sparse yellow streetlights made the darkness darker, and where someone always played a mysterious folk tune out of sight. In those dreams he didn't know whether he was waiting in fear for a vampire to consume him or hunting prey of his own.

In the Medina, their van weaved through the chaos of traffic, cars, people, bicycles, scooters, wheeled carts, and donkeys, miraculously not running into one another, as if it were a prechoreographed presentation. Ting rolled down the window, and the noise completed the picture: honks, footsteps, the moan of the wind, the tapping of raindrops on tin eaves, Arabic spoken so fast that it sounded like people were squabbling, merchants standing outside storefronts yelling different languages to tourists—English mainly, and French, but other languages, too, that she couldn't identify. She heard a man's voice saying "ni hao" right by her ear, but he must have walked by so fast that she missed the voice's owner. And the smells. There were hints of spices, a splash of ocean mixed with damp soil and grass, and faintly fishy. Then it was getting fishier, overwhelmingly fishier. Ting didn't realize they were passing an open-air seafood market until their van was in front of its crowded gate. She pressed the upward arrow on the window button. The moment the glass sealed the inside of the car, there was quiet again, as if they were submerged underwater.

"Look! That's Cafe Colon, from *The Sheltering Sky*," Ting called out.

Si-Bo turned his head to look but barely caught the exterior of the café.

"*The Sheltering Sky*." Almost five years ago, four books into Ting's career, she was invited to pen a new Chinese translation of Paul Bowles's *The Sheltering Sky* in celebration of its seventieth anniversary. Too busy to read Ting's book, Si-Bo watched Bertolucci's film adaptation with her instead. He found it ironic that they had arrived in the same place as the protagonists in the movie, hauling their dissolving marriage with them. Now Si-Bo repeated the name of the movie, as if attempting to imbue it with new meaning.

Their car came under a big, curvy arch with a pointy center and onto a narrow street that looked almost perpendicular to the horizon. The engine growled in frustration as it heaved them up the slope. Suddenly, the driver pulled the hand brake and the car halted on a slant. He got out of the car and, without a word, opened the door for Ting and Si-Bo. As Ting came out of the car, she saw a hand reaching above her in her peripheral vision. For a split second, with the unfriendly driver in such proximity, she was scared. Then she realized that he had simply pulled the hood of her parka over her head. It was still raining, and he didn't want her to get wet.

The driver unloaded their suitcases and rolled them to an opening on the side of the incline. Ting and Si-Bo looked up to see the three-story guesthouse atop the hilled street, and the thirty or forty steps that led up to it. Before Ting and Si-Bo could start strategizing how they would carry their suitcases up those harrowing steps, they saw the driver hurl one suitcase over his shoulder and begin ascending the stairs, his feet stomping the storied cobblestones in a steady rhythm all the way to the top. Then he ran back down, and did the same with the other suitcase.

They met him at the top of the hill. It was hard to tell whether the drops on his face were rain or sweat. Looking at him, Ting thought of her father, who would have been around the same age but much less brawny. Her father had been the gentlest man, and he hadn't smiled much either. Men of his generation had been brought up to be restrained and solemn. Maybe the driver was the same. How silly of her to have misunderstood him.

"Thank you *so much*." Ting couldn't think of anything kinder to say, so she smiled at him again. She thought she saw a faint smile rising at the corners of the driver's lips as he said goodbye, but she could have imagined it. He turned away and ran back to the car.

TING AND SI-BO met in a small liberal arts college in Maine, where there were fewer than ten Chinese students every year. Coming from Chinese megacities, they thought that the American college town was drab, cold, and oppressively lonely. Si-Bo was a year older, though his extra year at school hadn't earned him any more friends. American classmates considered him a reticent Chinese math nerd. They didn't know that Si-Bo was a sunny person in his mother tongue: he hadn't talked much in English because he had once overheard other Chinese students saying that his heavy accent embarrassed them. He understood English perfectly, but he was unable to get rid of his accent. He believed that the anatomy of his mouth was not made for that language. Ting, on the other hand, spoke English in a learned American accent and had studied literature with American classmates. Still, she was not American enough to date any of them. She didn't know the TV shows they grew up watching, the lyrics to pop music of the aughts, the brand names of candy, beer, and cigarettes that everyone bonded over, or the flirtatious jokes with which people hit on each other. She felt so stupid when she had to ask people to repeat their questions, then say, "Sorry, I don't know what that is," and she loathed feeling stupid. So it wasn't difficult for Ting and Si-Bo to find each other. They had started sleeping together during Ting's first Thanksgiving break, when all the American kids went home. The campus was desolate and the warmest place was in each other's beds, under each other's covers, inside each other's bodies. During the short time that they spent out of bed, they had gone to the back of the campus, where American couples liked to make out among a big patch of trees. In those days, the forest was theirs and theirs only. They reached their hands under layers of fabric and kissed until they couldn't feel their noses or toes. It was one of those situations where the sum of one plus one wasn't two: Ting's loneliness plus Si-Bo's loneliness equaled zero and it was loneliness no more, like some kind of magic trick. From the start, being with Ting defied mathematical rules and everything Si-Bo loved about them: their simplicity, clarity, and grace. Eleven years later, Si-Bo often thought that if there were an opposite of math, it would be marriage: messy, incalculable, and never equal on both sides.

When Si-Bo received his master's degree, they moved back to Shanghai together. Ting always wondered whether, if it wasn't for Si-Bo, whose parents wanted their son to stay close and inherit their family business someday, she would have wanted to stay in America. She had already started getting gigs as a translator for Chinese media during her year in New York and she loved the work. If she went back to Shanghai, she would probably get to translate books, which excited her. But she loved New York, she loved the surprises, possibilities, and serendipities that the city seemed to hold for those who called it home and for those in transit. In the end, the choice wasn't difficult, because it was impossible for her to obtain a work visa. She moved to Si-Bo's city, into the apartment that Si-Bo's parents had purchased for him. It didn't take long for Ting to become enamored with Shanghai. The city reminded her of New York, the humidity in the summer air, the coffee shops in the French Concession, the storied addresses where this writer or that artist lived, and the intangible qualities of the city, unpredictable, like a temperamental person, that moved her when she least expected it.

BY THE TIME Si-Bo woke up on the couch the next morning, it was eleven, and Ting had already left for the day. When he texted to ask where she was, she said that she preferred to walk around on her own but that they could meet for dinner at the restaurant Saveur de Poisson. Standing on their petite balcony and looking at the old cream-colored city, Si-Bo thought about what he should do. They usually went wherever Ting wanted to visit. Without her, he was clueless. He downloaded the travel app Mafengwo and swiped through the recommended destinations. The top sites were seaside spots that were too far to walk to, so he settled on a couple of places within the Medina, washed up, and headed downstairs.

On the first floor was a modest living room with three wooden tables and a kitchen that looked onto the living room through a square opening in the wall. The innkeeper Fatima was generous enough to pull out some breakfast items for Si-Bo—Moroccan pastries, olives, fig jam—that she had already put away for the day. She asked him if he wanted tea.

"What tea?" His English was rusty. He felt embarrassed uttering those rounder vowels that sat deeper in his throat than Mandarin did.

"Mint tea. It's Moroccan special," said Fatima, her friendly face accentuated by her blue hijab.

Si-Bo thanked her. A few minutes later, Fatima brought out a silver teapot, its body covered in curvy lines moving and crossing in relief, and its handle wrapped in a delicate piece of purple embroidery. She warned Si-Bo not to burn himself. Si-Bo said okay and let out a quiet snicker that Fatima didn't seem to notice. Si-Bo knew that she was only being thoughtful, but he couldn't help but feel offended. He was Chinese. Did she think he didn't know how to drink tea? He could imagine his American classmates from college, attracted to the intricate pattern on the teapot, touching it with their bare fingers and yelling, "Ouch!" They knew nothing of tea or teapots. Their tea came in bags, the worst tea ground in the worst way.

"Where are you going today?" Fatima asked from the kitchen.

"I think I'm just going to walk around."

"Do you like sunset?"

He loved sunset, how the sun kindled the clouds. It was at once the same anywhere in the world and particular to each place, varying just slightly in indescribable, unsentimental ways.

"The best place to watch sunset in Tangier is Café Hafa," said Fatima, pleased with Si-Bo's affirmative answer. "It's walking distance from here."

"Great. Thank you." Si-Bo smiled.

Si-Bo got lost in the maze of the Medina for the whole afternoon, wandering into alleys connected by low arches and irrational turns, only, at the bottom of an unnamed hill, to be surprised when the landscape opened up again onto a cemetery full of trees with stray cats on one side and a white Christian church on the other. He overheard a woman with a North American accent talking about how the architecture had ended up in some famous painter's "kaleidoscopic body of work." When he came out of the church complex, Si-Bo stumbled upon a street market and walked through rows of farmers in big hats who sat cross-legged behind their baskets of fruits and vegetables and cast their aloof, solicitous eyes onto passersby. Then he hit a tranquil patch, and a regal, European-style château presented itself. He wondered if this was where Port and Kit stayed in *The Sheltering Sky*. He took a photo of it with his phone and continued walking.

When he felt thirsty, he stopped for some pomegranate juice for ten dirhams. The merchant, who looked barely eighteen, hand-pressed three pomegranates through the juicer and poured the juice into an actual glass—no plastic. Si-Bo thought Ting would have been thrilled about that. It wasn't that he didn't believe in climate change (not a phrase Ting would use, for she believed it to be something much more imminent, much more disastrous than politicians' inaccurate, manipulative use of the word "change"). He recycled when he could. But if saving plastics, minimizing waste, or whatever Ting insisted on doing cost him comfort or convenience, he wouldn't bother. In this moment, though, standing next to the juice cart and appreciating the flow of the crowd as his lips reddened from the sweet, acidic elixir, he didn't mind the glass. It was the best juice he had ever tasted. Si-Bo took out another ten-dirham bill and asked for seconds.

When he arrived at Café Hafa, around six, the open-air rooftop was packed with people waiting to be seated. The popular spot seemed as disorganized as the streets of the Medina. It took Si-Bo a while before he got the attention of a server and was led to a table already occupied by a hip Moroccan couple in their twenties. They glanced at Si-Bo in a friendly way without pausing their conversation. He noticed that the woman—similarly, in fact, to many local women here—was not wearing her headscarf. He didn't know much about Islam, but somehow this put him more at ease. He ordered a mint tea, the kind he'd liked in the morning, and looked out at the ocean. Café Hafa was built against the side of a cliff and laid out in multiple levels, like rice terraces. From where Si-Bo sat, he could see the sun setting over the ocean toward his left, and in the distance, across the strait, the land of Spain. After hours of meandering between the walls of the Medina, which always seemed to be closing in on him from both sides, this high, open vista of the ocean was a liberating change of scenery.

Ting would love it here, he thought. It was a habit of his to wish for her when he had something worth sharing: a good plate of food, a stunning view, a vision of a future he was willing to work for. If that's not love, then what is, Si-Bo wanted to ask someone. He wanted answers. If Ting were here, maybe he'd work up the courage to have a serious talk with her again, in front of the ocean, basking in the golden glow of the North African sun. Maybe a change of heart would take a chance and pay them a visit. He took a few photos of the view but had no one to send them to. He tried to post them on WeChat but couldn't think of a caption, so he closed the app without saving a draft. He put his phone away and scanned the café for something else to dwell on: items on people's tables, tourists taking photos of each other, white square tiles with intricate patterns, trees one level below whose species he couldn't quite place. And then, sitting among all of these strange things, there was something familiar—or rather, someone. There, as if the magic lamp had granted Si-Bo's wish without his asking, was Ting. She was pulling her gray scarf off her head and chuckling with two girls at her table as she ruffled the silky fabric around her neck, almost blushing. Her head had been covered; that must have been why he hadn't seen her before. He wished he had been prepared for the sight of her. She looked happy, and it hurt him to see her happy in his absence. Si-Bo couldn't remember the last time he saw her laugh like that. She was listening intently to one of the girls; now she started speaking, too. Their conversation looked earnest.

The next thing he knew, he was tapping Ting on the shoulder. She turned around, surprised, and for a moment she looked as if she was going to say something to him, but she didn't. Instead, she asked the girls if Si-Bo could sit with them. They welcomed Si-Bo and introduced themselves. One of them wore a blue sweatshirt that read *KANYE ATTITUDE WITH DRAKE FEELINGS.*

"They go to college here. Imane is studying to be a lawyer, and Sairish is studying to be a doctor. Isn't that amazing?" Ting said to Si-Bo, in English, as if she were their proud older sister. Imane and Sairish giggled shyly.

"That *is* amazing," Si-Bo said. "What were you talking about? I don't mean to interrupt."

Si-Bo's question was directed to no one in particular. Imane and Sairish seemed to assume Ting would answer, but Ting was taking a long time to sip her tea, insisting on silence.

Finally, Imane spoke. "We were asking Ting how the pandemic was like in China, because we read everything was really strict there."

"And I was also asking her if China was going to find out how the virus happened," Sairish added. "After the pandemic, I'm kind of thinking maybe I can be, what is it called . . ." She paused to think, but the right word didn't come to her. "Like doctors that focus on pandemics like this. We are probably going to have more and more of pandemics in the future." She made a sad face as if she was completing her sentence with an emoji. "And what happened in China was terrible, I'm sorry."

Other than the occasional emails with foreign clients, and group Zoom calls where he only had to listen, Si-Bo hadn't had a real-time conversation in English for many years. He wasn't sure if he was up for broaching this topic in a language that he couldn't command with confidence. The Moroccan girls spoke English with a certain downward intonation that must have come from Arabic, and it took Si-Bo some getting used to. Meanwhile Ting was looking at him in a way that he couldn't instantly decipher. She probably wanted him to keep his mouth shut. But this conversation, which Ting and he had had so many times since the beginning of the pandemic, wasn't simply between the two of them now. They were talking to these girls who weren't Chinese. Si-Bo felt compelled to speak his mind, not just for himself but for his country.

"The Chinese lockdown was why we had the virus for only three months, while America has been so bad for two years!" Realizing that he had raised his voice, Si-Bo swallowed and started again. "We are from Shanghai, and the virus almost never made it there, not at first. Yes, then we had a few, but it was all from people coming in from other countries, and whenever there was a case it was contained right away. The lockdown and the quarantine, it was the only way, the right way."

Ting was looking down at her lap and picking at the rougher skin around her nails. She had known exactly what Si-Bo was going to say before the words came out of his mouth. She didn't know why she'd looked at him the way that she had. Perhaps it was a dare, to see if he would stand by his convictions in front of foreigners. Now that he had said it, she debated whether she should let it slide, and steer the conversation toward something unimportant and pleasant, or, once again, push back. They had fought over the Chinese government's authoritarian tactics again and again, and over countless other issues: their respective gender roles, the censorship she faced in publishing, the internet bullying of a feminist comedienne, deals at his workplace that made the rich ultrarich and worked the poor to literal death. Whether to buy from big corporations whose algorithms exploited their employees; what, if anything, to do about the doomed planet; the omnipresent surveillance. Over Hong Kong, Xinjiang, Taiwan, over America, over *Wolf Warrior*, over boycotting *Nomadland*, over the military parade on National Day, over the disappearances of activists and journalists, over changes to the constitution, and so on, and so on. Ting couldn't quite pinpoint when Si-Bo had changed. No single event had altered his perspective, as in the clean narrative of a movie. At first, she'd thought Si-Bo had just been poisoned, and if she could find the antidote, if she could pull him back to her side, if she could prove to him that his sources of information were unreliable, if the people they called friends were suffering as a result of what he believed to be right, if she appealed to him as his loving wife, she could save him, save their marriage. But nothing worked. Then it had occurred to her that perhaps it was their country that had changed, but to blame the government or a certain population for their divorce was a stretch, and a dissatisfactory one at that. Then she thought perhaps that Si-Bo had been the same person all along, and it was she who hadn't known whom she married. At any rate, it was suffocating. As if someone had their grip on her throat day and night, the oxygen in her private, domestic space slowly being sucked out, indistinguishable from the repressive air engulfing the public sphere.

Fuck it. They were getting a divorce. There was no reason she should hold back any longer.

Ting glanced up at Imane and Sairish, who looked taken aback. They were looking at her, holding her responsible in some way. She said, "Remember I was trying to explain young Chinese people called 'Little Pink'? I forgot to mention that I'm married to one."

"Oh, I didn't know you guys are married," Sairish said, exchanging a look with Imane. The two girls were catching up to their new Chinese friends now.

"It's not important," Ting said, "because—"

"We're getting divorced." Si-Bo thought he might as well beat her to it, if that was what she wanted everyone to know.

"His always trying to finish my sentences is only part of the reason."

Si-Bo wished he could make jokes in English, like Ting, who was sharing a conspiratorial smirk with the girls.

She turned to him. "See, that's not what I was gonna say. I was saying that it's not important because what we were talking about, the pandemic, was more important." Ting continued the conversation in English not only for the sake of their spectators but also for the uncharitable pleasure of taking advantage of his weakness.

"You say the lockdown and the quarantine was the right way, but at what cost? You know the same things I know. A paralyzed boy was starved to death because his only caretaker was sent to mandatory quarantine. Pregnant women couldn't get to hospitals because their residential complexes had just one *suspected* case. People kept getting stuck away from their homes because lockdowns happened overnight without any notice—roads closed, all forms of transportation halted. Small businesses never got any government help. Even just a few months ago, they were putting down people's cats and dogs because their owners were forced into mandatory quarantine. What right do they have to kill those innocent animals? Not to mention Chinese overseas haven't been able to see their families for over two years. Even if you're recovered, they test your antibodies and make it impossible to come in. You remember what happened to Yi-Lun." Ting turned to the girls to explain. "One of my best friends, she couldn't even come home when her dad died."

"That's crazy!" Imane gasped. "And they killed people's cats? How did the cats have anything to do with anything?"

"Animals can get sick, too," Si-Bo said with authority.

"He doesn't care about dogs and cats," Ting said dismissively.

"I think humans give it to them, though," Sairish said, picking her phone up from the table to check.

"So, you tell them, how was any of it for the good of the country?" Ting demanded of Si-Bo.

Si-Bo didn't look at Sairish or Imane. He kept his eyes on Ting. "It was good for the health and safety of the majority of the people, people like you and me. You benefited from it, too. Show some appreciation."

"I didn't *want* other people to sacrifice their lives for mine. But there wasn't anything I could do about that, was there? That's the whole fucking problem, isn't it? *That's* why we're getting a divorce. At least I can decide what to do with my own fucking marriage. And please don't talk like you and I are the same. It's obvious we're not."

Nobody, not even Ting herself, could have foreseen the segue into the topic of their marriage. Imane and Sairish defaulted to awkward speechlessness, looking far out at the horizon.

Si-Bo spoke again. "So you'd rather be in America and get COVID, then? You think they care about people like you? Maybe you forget what it felt like to live like second-class citizens, but I haven't."

"You always ask me that, as if it's even a logical question. Whatever America does or doesn't do is beside the point. Neither China nor America has to be right, or better. America is also fucked up, just in a different way."

"Exactly. Our system proved to be the greatest at reacting to national emergencies like this pandemic."

"You're ridiculous. Everything with you is about how our system is superior, how we won the war against COVID. It's like the whole country has amnesia. What about Wuhan? They knew it for more than a month and told no one. We still don't know how many people died. Nobody talks about it. It's all victory, celebration, the greatest people, the greatest country. Aren't you sick of it?" Ting felt a soreness climbing up to the top of her nose, and she breathed in to let the fresh air wash through it. She was not going to cry. How had her sunset with mint tea and sweet Moroccan girls at Café Hafa, where the Beatles and the Rolling Stones had once sat and chatted about sex, drugs, and rock 'n' roll, turned into this?

The sun had dipped under the horizon while Si-Bo and Ting were not paying attention. Now the clouds stirred, gently as a strawberry milkshake, as the sky darkened by the minute. Everything in sight was losing definition.

Then Si-Bo spoke in Mandarin, almost startling the girls.

"Ting, why can't you just love your country? Why do you have to hate it so much?"

"I don't. You know that. Love and hate are not mutually exclusive."

"You hate me. You've said so."

"I hate how you make me feel. I hate that I feel the most alone when I'm with you."

"What you said about hate and love not being mutually exclusive—does that also apply to us?"

"I don't know."

Ting didn't think there was anything else for her to say. She wasn't going to say "I don't love you anymore" as if she were the heroine of a melodrama. It wouldn't be accurate, either. It wasn't that she didn't love him anymore; it was that she couldn't. She could only imagine that Si-Bo felt the same.

Si-Bo stood up, freeing both of them.

Not long after Si-Bo left Café Hafa, Ting apologized to Imane and Sairish, and left, too. She went to Saveur de Poisson, as planned, and had a big Moroccan dinner on her own. When she came back to their room, neither Si-Bo nor his suitcase was there. She fell into a coma-like slumber and woke up the next morning in the same clothes that she'd worn the day before, which now smelled like salty sweat and smoked fish, cooled anger, and expired sorrow.

ON TING'S LAST day in Tangier, she took a day trip to the dreamy blue village Chefchaouen, where she ran into to a group of local women drumming and singing in the street, in celebration of something, the exact nature of which she never came to learn. She sat in the village square listening to the afternoon call to prayer emitted from the mosque's loudspeaker. That night, she rode an overnight train to Marrakech, the starting point for her journey into the Sahara. The rhythmic clickety-clack of the old train wheels rolling over the rail joints kept her up all night. Lying awake in the faint, flickering beams of lamps along both sides of the track, Ting admitted to herself that, everywhere she'd gone, she'd wondered if she would see Si-Bo. For all she knew, Si-Bo might already have gotten on a flight back to Shanghai. She didn't know what difference it made, him being in the country or not. She had planned to travel all by herself in the first place. But now that Si-Bo had come and gone, it was as if he had left a dimple on her heart that she couldn't fill with anything else. It was not even that she actually wanted to see Si-Bo, or that she minded roaming solo. It was that the circumstances under which Si-Bo had left seemed imperfect, unfinished somehow. She felt abandoned, though she understood none of what had happened as abandonment. They'd spent a precious decade with each other—if not the most precious decade of their lives. Didn't they deserve a proper farewell?

The sun in Marrakech burned Ting's skin in a way that was unfamiliar to her, but she managed to find shade under the wooden canopies that hung over the souks. As she was driven through the Atlas Mountains to the Saharan village of Merzouga, the sun got lower and harsher, the air thicker and dryer. It would take two days to get to her camp in the desert, and the tour guide, Reda, with whom she had been in contact before the trip, brought his friend Simo with him. They spoke Arabic to one another and she couldn't understand a word of it. During the first hours, it crossed her mind more than once that they could easily drive her to a remote place—the whole drive looked remote—and rob her, rape her, and/or kill her.

Then they started talking to her. They were both twenty-nine years old. Reda was from Merzouga, so he liked driving tourists into the desert: he got to see his parents and stay in his childhood house. Simo was Berber. Reda had brought him on the trip to show him the route and scenic stops along the way, so Simo could start driving tourists on his own soon. It was a profitable gig if one liked driving and meeting people from around the world. Ting asked them questions about Morocco, Islam, and the history of the Berber people; they asked Ting about her school days in America, her work as a translator, and if she was married. Ting decided to tell them that she was, and felt the two men treating her differently afterward—with more respect, perhaps. Si-Bo was there, protecting her, without physically being there, without even knowing. He would be happy to know that, she thought. How sad it was, being a woman in a man's world, but she was relieved to feel safe. Fortunately, Reda and Simo didn't probe further into her marriage, so she didn't have to make up any lies. The three of them stuck to less personal topics. It felt good to talk about, think about, anything else.

THE MOMENT TING knew they were officially in the Sahara was unmistakable.

"Here we go. As-Sahra!" Reda declared. Their four-wheel Jeep leaped off the gravel road and started swimming through loose sand.

Ting bounced up and down in the back seat, but smoothly, not in the jerky way one does when one hits a speed bump on a city

street. She felt adrenaline bubbling in her body, making her nervous, and almost confusing her, but exhilarating her all the same.
It was all warm sand, as far as her eyes could see, infinitely flat,
infinitely edgeless, and the heat waves vibrated, boiling up in the
space above the ground.

"What does 'Sahara' mean?" she asked Reda and Simo.

"It just means 'desert' in Arabic."

"Really?" Ting always supposed the word "Sahara" meant
something grand, something profound, something that would give
her life new perspective. Now that she thought about it, the meaning of words was often transformed when they were adopted by
other languages. It happened all the time.

"There are no marks or anything here." Ting looked back to see
the shallow prints left by their rugged wheels, destined to disappear in minutes. "How do you know where we are going?"

"No need for marks. I grew up in this desert," said Reda,
unfazed.

"It's like you have a superpower," said Ting.

The two boys cracked up, gleefully repeating, "Superpower!"

Ting closed her eyes, swaying with the car to keep her balance.
The dryness in the air was already baking her throat.

Camp was a few tents standing firmly in the middle of the desert. Reda told her that the people at the camp would take her on
a camel ride in the afternoon, and that dinner would be included.
He made a joke about how she wouldn't have anywhere else to eat.
He and Simo would pick her up tomorrow morning, after sunrise,
and drive her to Fez. Before he drove away, he reminded Ting not
to forget to look at the stars at night.

Ting settled her luggage in her tent and waited in the back of the camp. High dunes rose in the distance. It was difficult to gauge how far they were.

"That's Erg Chebbi," the camp attendant, Saïd, told her.

"Erg?"

"Like a sea of sand dunes," he explained, his right hand tracing the curves of the dunes in the air.

"It's beautiful," Ting said. "Is there anyone else coming on the camel ride?"

"Yeah, we have three other guests. They went to Merzouga village for the market. An Italian couple, and a guy, Chinese. They should be back soon."

"A Chinese guy by himself?" Ting had to ask. "What does he look like?"

"About my height. Quiet guy. Very nice. He's here for two nights already." Saïd squinted, trying to recall if there were more details that he could share. "He really love our shepherd. We got a puppy here a few months ago. I let him feed the dog every day."

Si-Bo was about Saïd's height. But would he get along with a dog? Ting couldn't be certain.

WHEN TING HEARD a car approaching, she hurried to the front of the camp, so that when Si-Bo got out of the car, Ting was there waiting. He had expected to see her today, but he hadn't prepared what to say. He walked toward Ting and she walked toward him.

"I wasn't sure it would be you." Ting stopped before him at arm's length. They didn't hug. "You don't like dogs."

"I never did, but guess I do now. People change."

"What are you doing here?"

"You think I would abandon you just like that?"

"You didn't abandon me."

"I wanted to get out of Tangier, and I knew you were coming to the desert. I thought it might do me good, clear my thoughts a little, so I came early."

"It's surreal, isn't it?"

They looked around, as though, in each other's presence, they were seeing the desert for the first time again.

"You coming on the camel ride?" Ting asked in a cheery tone.

Ting, Si-Bo, and the Italian couple wrapped their hair and covered their faces as instructed, straddled their gentle but inscrutable camels, and set out toward the dunes.

Saïd led the caravan on foot. They trekked for a while, then got off at the bottom of a high dune and climbed up to the peak. The Italian couple sat down and leaned into each other. Ting and Si-Bo planted themselves away from the couple, each hugging their legs into their chests, taking care to leave a virtuous distance between them. The sun was setting over the rolling hills of sand.

"So did the desert help you clear your thoughts?" Ting asked.

"I don't know yet." Si-Bo paused for a few seconds before speaking again. "It makes me feel very small. Maybe a lot of the things I cared about don't matter as much as I think."

Si-Bo didn't know what, exactly, he was referring to. It was just a feeling. Ting nodded, not knowing what he meant, and not wanting to know more. In this moment, sand was all they saw; silence was all they heard. Nothing else mattered, and there was nothing more to say. It was as if they had finally reached a tacit understanding. Tonight they would gaze at the stars. Tomorrow they might fight like there was no tomorrow. In three days they would be back in their homeland. In another fifteen, they might meet again at the marriage bureau and go home with their divorce certificates. A year or two after that, they might lose touch. In thirty years, they might start asking themselves if there was any meaning in fighting with anyone. In fifty years, they might forget each other's names and the name of the country where they once rode camels in a great desert. Or none of that would happen, not in the way they expected, because life wasn't like that. Here and now, they were Si-Bo and Ting, Ting and Si-Bo, watching the daylight pass over the Sahara, to the other side of the world.

Mengyin Lin is a Chinese writer living in the United States. Mandarin is her mother tongue and she writes in English as her second language. She holds an MFA in fiction from Brooklyn College and a BFA in film from New York University. Her fiction is published in *Epiphany, Joyland, Fence,* and *Pleiades* and her nonfiction in *The New York Times.* She is the winner of the *Epiphany* 2022 Breakout Writers Prize.

Editors' Note

With our shared love for language-focused, viscerally immediate stories, the fiction team at *Waxwing* sent a series of messages to each other about a submission that stunned us. Sonia Feldman's "Outgrowth" is the story of a scientist who chooses isolation from the broader world and from her otherwise all-male cohort on a closed botanical study site, but whose plants—and whose overwhelming mother, over the phone—keep her company as she analyzes what she means, and what her body means, to herself after a recent trauma. The language was specific and so sharply structured as to immerse us, so that when the realism of the piece gave way to a broader understanding of what language can do, we were wholly present for that broadening. That feeling—of being fully present when being shown a world more expansive than our current understanding—is what we're after, and when we can bring it to our readers through stories like "Outgrowth," we're thrilled.

During the editorial process for "Outgrowth," Feldman used another word that really stuck with me: that the protagonist, though many ways cocooned exactly as she intends, is ultimately "porous." Although this story has no specific pandemic references, I think the questions it poses about what it means to be porous as a woman among men, a human among plants, other animals, and other humans, and then again as a reader of literary fiction in a world awash with verbal information are also timely. As the Fall 2022 issue, where "Outgrowth" appears, marked the end of Fiction Editor Tara Zambrano's tenure at *Waxwing*, the piece joins the collection of fiction she gathered these past few years to remind us that literature is about place, time, and most of all, how language shapes the way we interact with these.

Rashi Rohatgi and Hairol Ma, Fiction Coeditors
Waxwing

Outgrowth

Sonia Feldman

"SOMETHING IS CHANGING IN THE GREENHOUSE," I tell my mother. She starts to ask what—but the phone drops. Service is shaky in the facility. When she calls back, it takes a couple of rings for me to convince myself to pick up again. First thing she wants to know is if I've been able to get my hours reduced or secure a week of vacation. It's in my contract, she reminds me, the right to take days off. Have I asked? Have I made them look at the calendar? Aren't I lonely?

"We haven't seen you in months," she says.

She's not likely to see me for the rest of the year either, but it's easier between us if I tell her truths only a little bit at a time. Besides, I'm sweaty and impatient from my day working with the plants. I wipe my hands on my legs, and my fingers leave behind streaks of sticky orange pollen. My room has a sink but no toilet. I wash my hands with the phone gripped between my ear and my shoulder and placate my mother as best I can. I remind her that I'm focused on my work; the plants keep me company; I'm fine; I'm normal; I have to go; someone needs something important from me.

"Okay sweetie, we love you," she says.

I kick off my clothes and lie on the floor of my room in my underwear until dinner. Air conditioning hums through the vent in my ceiling. I'm only ever able to hear the loving in her voice once we're off the phone.

The whole team eats dinner together in front of an enormous television. The screen is as large as the length of the table, and we sit in a U around it like a class observing a presentation. John stands up to make a blameless joke we all laugh at. He has no official authority over the group but is its de facto leader.

There are eight of us, young scientists hired straight out of graduate school to tend a population of flowering plants. The work is physically demanding, offers no possibility of advancement, and can't ever be leveraged into publishable scientific papers. We've all signed away the right to talk officially about what happens here. On the other hand, to work at the facility, each of us went through a vetting process that grants a level of government security clearance. When our contracts expire, we can use that clearance to apply to other, more desirable positions. Besides, working here does pay better than being an adjunct for some university.

We eat in silence with the lights off and our eyes on the television, an animated series in which it is always nighttime. There is never any talk between us, any asking after each other. I couldn't tell you where the other scientists are from, hardly have a grip on their last names even. I know little about the people with whom I've spent these past months of exclusive company. Around a half an hour later, my coworkers cautiously rise from their seats. They leave the table one or two at a time, taking their plates to the kitchen and pleading exhaustion. I make eye contact with each of them as they leave, let my eyes unfurl over their faces like sheets flung out over a bed.

When they're all up and gone, I leave the darkened kitchen.

The fluorescent white light of the hallway stings my eyes temporarily. I blink my way to the communal showers, which I'm allowed to use alone by silent group consensus—the only woman here. Small metal showerheads line the rectangular room. Each allots only a few minutes of hot water per hour, so I turn them on in succession, moving around the perimeter of the room and cranking the handle of a new faucet whenever the previous runs cold. I'm never reprimanded for this behavior. I suppose no one has ever wanted to turn me in.

I loosen the first faucet and imagine the scene I know to be gathering. The men, in their nightclothes, are returning to the kitchen together, where they take their same seats at the table, perhaps run their hands through their hair, and then watch spectacularly conventional porn while I take my shower. This happens every night. They must have brought physical discs with them to the facility—our internet use is monitored—or perhaps they're unashamed. Through a vent in the ceiling of the shower room float urgent, feminine moans. I listen closely while I shampoo my hair and pick up, too, the clear sounds of my coworkers talking. Their voices reach me, seven men having what by all means sounds like a routine, personable discussion.

This is what most astonished me when I heard them for the first time, several weeks after beginning work here—the everyday intimacy of their conversation, its even keel. They don't talk over one another. I hear only one male voice at a time. There are never any arguments. There is never any shouting, nor any sounds of love or pleasure, nor even an accumulating or climactic silence. Once, I could have sworn, I heard them discussing their parents, vacations they'd taken as families when they were children. Someone spoke of a brother dying inebriated in a car crash, but I've never known which one of them.

Sometimes I cut my shower erratically short for the hell of it. Today, I take my time, sigh in the hissing heat, my hands at my thighs. Strands of my hair run toward the drain like a pack of black threads. When at last I do turn off the water from the final showerhead, the voices disappear almost simultaneously. I dry off in the adjoining locker room and then just stand for a while in front of the only mirror in the facility, remembering what I look like. My face has new shadows. My body is too small. I haven't tried to catch the men because I'm afraid they'll stop.

I CAN HARDLY sleep here. I tend to just drift through the hours in half consciousness and wake up in the morning with my hands on my stomach, feeling for what isn't there. I eat breakfast alone, no television, and then exit the residential wing of the facility as soon as its doors unlock at seven. In a designated antechamber, I don my protective suit, which is made of a heavy, synthetic material and has a clear hood. I put on my boots, green and knee high, and an enormous pair of gardening gloves that extend past my elbows like evening wear. Then I fill up my watering tank from the spout of distilled water and mix in the prescribed amount of nutrient powder. The tanks are made of a high-grade plastic. From the body of each extends a long tube attached to a hand mister. I heave mine against my hip and walk into the greenhouse.

It's a great, domed room, a long hallway of green—five rows of plants extend like fingers from the entrance to the far end of the room, half a mile away. The greenhouse's arcing walls are made of frosted glass, behind which gigantic grow lamps beam diffused light onto the nearly five thousand plants lined up on the tables below. We grow only a single species here, a small white flower whose name we've never been told and is not listed on any document I've seen.

The flower has five small, gossamer petals that purse like a mouth around a cluster of electric orange stamens. The stamens are thin as strands of hair and nearly ten times the length of the petals from which they emerge. Each plant requires, for its size, an unusually large and robust root system to bloom. We grow them in deep, black plastic troughs of soil. Buds fall off dead if our care regimen falters by even a day.

The following limited information was made available to us in the orientation packet we received when we took the job. The species was initially assumed to be perfect (each flower having *both* male and female organs) and therefore self-pollinating. However, experimentation revealed that any given individual plant of the species requires a second to produce seeds. The plants must then be imperfect (flowers having *either* male or female organs) and dioecious (plants producing *either* male or female flowers).

But it proved impossible to conclude which plants were producing female flowers and which were producing male. All of the flowers are visually identical. Both organs are present, but only one is active. Efforts to systematically determine the sex of an individual plant by manual pollination yielded erratic results. Plants that reliably produced seeds for several cycles suddenly stopped doing so and became able to pollinate other female plants instead.

The scientists who conducted these investigations determined that the species is actually dichogamous: the sex of the plant fluctuates throughout its life cycle, possibly in relation to external conditions. The nature of those conditions was not expanded upon in the packet. A pattern that can accurately predict the sex of a flower at a given point in its life cycle has not been found.

Given these complications, we use an air circulation system to pollinate the plants. Vents blow a soft wind through the greenhouse, sweeping orange pollen from flower to flower. This system prevents us from tracking the parentage of new seeds, but then it isn't our job to study their genealogy or even to study the plants at all. Our mandate is the tending and expansion of an existing population of flowers.

Since the first two weeks of work, during which we proved ourselves competent enough in the tasks assigned, we haven't had a single in-person visitor. Our progress is monitored through the digital reports we submit. We receive no feedback beyond a graph that tracks the current plant population against expected growth. That's why we've been hired—ostensibly as scientists but really as caretakers, highly educated grounds people.

I walk to the farthest row, my mister against my hip. An enormous internal watering system showers the plants every hour, but the nutrient mix has to be delivered manually to prevent overgrowth. I begin to spray the plants one tray at a time. With my right hand, I click the mister open and shut. After a few minutes, I want to switch sides. My right hand aches, but my left is too weak to be useful. Whenever I switch to my left side, I can only clamp the mister shut a few times before the spring-loaded pressure tires the hand out completely and I have to change back. The ache is familiar after many days of this work, and there is a kind of satisfaction in allowing myself to be subsumed by it. I step and mist, step and mist. I grow hot in my suit, and my breath collects against the inside of my protective hood. I quickly lift it and wipe free the condensation.

A couple of hours later, the men walk in. I must be four or five city blocks from the entrance. I can see them conferring seriously. Most often, they talk about developments in the field and debate the merit of recently published papers based solely on information available in the abstracts. At least three of them wear glasses, but which three seems to change depending on the day. Eventually, I wave at them and they wave back, looking for all the world like a set of figurines.

I call my mom on the phone at night. I want to watch a movie, and I've forgotten the password to our shared account on the video-streaming service. She seizes the opportunity to tell me—I shouldn't be alone for so long after losing a baby. Wouldn't I be better off at home, where she could take care of me. I hold a long silence between us—point it at her like a knife.

"I'm not alone," I say eventually.

"Those men don't count."

"I know they don't."

I hang up without the password. In bed, absence clamors through my body like a flock of birds.

THE OTHERS MOVE through the greenhouse as a unit. They split the caretaking tasks between themselves and perform them in an assembly line. One misting, one pruning, one with a bin for seeds, and so on. This arrangement should, in theory, improve their efficiency, and it's true, I never see them wasting time. They don't dally. They don't stand around at leisure. They all have stiff, excellent posture. Still, I routinely outstrip their numbers, see to more plants, process more seeds, submit more robust reports at the end of the day and then again in summary at the end of the week. I've read their reports—entirely formal and accurate. Perhaps it's this intermediate competence that unsettles me. Perhaps it's their unwillingness to work alone. I don't like to be near them. I can't think when they're around.

So I bury myself within the greenhouse. Easy, as I'm not particularly tall. The more mature plants, seated on top of their tables, reach my shoulders. We're supposed to prune them, trim the long-necked stems that droop into the aisles, but I allow various corridors of the greenhouse to grow close with foliage. The men don't notice. They leave the farthest and least convenient reaches of the room to my exclusive care. Walking among these aisles, I imagine I'm near invisible.

My water tank weighs heavily against my hip, so I put it down on the ground to get a better look at the two trays of plants in front of me. They're both in full bloom, the pursed white petals of the small flowers practically glowing against the background of their robust green leaves. The flowers in both trays have turned to face each other. Their stems strain toward one another. Their flower heads almost brush faces. Their viscerally orange stamens join. The plants look like two gusts of wind from opposite directions have blown them into a colliding peak.

I don't know how the plants behave in nature or if they can even survive outside the controlled environment of the greenhouse. Here, they exhibit positive tropic behavior: the flowers gently rotate throughout the day, growth toward a stimulus. Such a stimulus is normally environmental, but the environment here is static: the temperature and humidity of the greenhouse stable, the air blowing through the circulation system continuously, the diffused light of the grow lamps beaming down evenly at all hours. Instead, the flowers orient themselves toward each other, seeking pollination partners.

I'm the only one in the group who pays the plants' behavior any mind. The men don't care. None of us are paid to care. Still, I take down the identification numbers for the two trays in front of me. I'll include a description of their behavior in my daily report. The severity of their rotation is unusual. In most cases, the tropism is subtle, hardly visible. It's never uniform. You never walk into the greenhouse to find the flowers all facing in one direction or even large swaths of them moving cohesively. An unknown instinct directs each individual plant to turn and face some other.

I straighten, my hand bracing my back, and heave my water tank up from the ground to resume my rhythmic misting, step and mist, step and mist. I feel my eyes glaze over and welcome the familiar sensation, the absence from myself. When I'm working with the flowers, a window in my mind flings open. My thoughts, like springtime animals, bound through the aperture and into the gaping distance. Something like relief.

Then the men round a corner and stand unexpectedly before me. It's easy to lose track of each other in here. Our protective hoods muffle sound, and the height of the mature plants limits visibility across the aisles. But their sudden appearance feels purposeful, malignant. The seven of them rarely work this far from the door.

"Nomi," John says.

"Hello," I say.

The walkway is too narrow for all of us to congregate together, so John faces me and the remaining six hover behind him in pairs like school children, eyeing the overgrown aisle. The orange stamens of the flowers like long tongues encroach against their chests, slide against their necks.

"I received a message this morning."

"They wrote to you?" I can't help asking. "Was there any mention of the increased tropic activity?" Instances of which I had been including almost every day in my notes.

He shakes his head, and light from one of the lamps bounces off his protective hood. The surface goes momentarily opaque, obscuring his face, and I wince from the sharp brightness.

"None—they asked that we prepare a greater than usual number of seeds for pickup tomorrow."

The seeds we harvest are carefully dried, to prevent molding, and then either propagated into new flowers or else packaged and stored in the seed depository. Weekly, a portion of those stored seeds are removed to another facility. To what end, we don't know. Why the plants merit such large-scale and regulated production has never been explained to us, the purpose of our work undisclosed.

Nor have its risks been elucidated. They gave us instructions for protective equipment—the outfits we wear, the hoods and gloves and shoes that don't leave the greenhouse antechamber, and none of it to be removed while working within the greenhouse itself. But the nature of the threat the plants could potentially pose has been left unmentioned, and while we are asked to wear protective gear, our suits are not airtight and the door into the greenhouse does not vacuum seal.

The plant has potential as a soporific agent.

I read that in a footnote of the orientation materials without further explanation. I haven't felt so much as sleepy in months. I think the truth is they're not entirely sure what the risks are. Better to be on the safe side, assign us equipment, but I have to imagine that if the threat were particularly serious, they would have found people more qualified to do the work. If there were a real risk, wouldn't they be obligated to tell us about it? I could be wrong. Perhaps that's why the job came with such thorough and appealing health insurance.

While we're talking, I notice movement behind John. Two of the others have taken out their shears and begun to prune the long-necked flowers leaning into the aisle. The discarded blossoms drop into the men's buckets untouched. I know they will be incinerated with the rest of the day's debris. It's difficult for me to concentrate.

I try to regain my ground, straighten, and say, "Leave me alone to work then. If we need to process that number of seeds—I doubt I'll even have time for a shower."

Feet behind John do shuffle at the mention, so I take my victory and flee deeper into the greenhouse. I spend the next four hours in a kind of trance, moving from plant to plant and collecting the seed pods that represent the final stage of the plants' life cycle. Some split open when I drop them into my bin and seeds spill out. I miss dinner, spend the night carefully preparing the seeds for the next day's retrieval. Eventually, I collapse into bed exhausted and unbathed. It does please me to think I've deprived them of something.

———

OUR PROPAGATION EFFORTS are temporarily halted. Instead of planting new trays, the entire team is to focus on collecting and processing the seeds of existing mature plants. The change in routine makes me uneasy. I call my mother to complain. She asks if this means I'll be allowed to take a vacation soon—she's relentless.

In her quietest voice, she promises, "I won't say a word. I won't say a thing. If you come home, I'll be perfect."

I put my hand over my mouth to catch a sob.

"I'll call again soon."

A week into our new mandate, my bin is nearly full of seeds. I see the men in the distance exiting the greenhouse and wander into one of the nursery aisles to admire the neat rows of new life. The slim, verdant shoots look so small in the wide black troughs of soil where they will spend their entire lives. The plants are never repotted nor their bins rearranged. They expand until their containers limit further increase. It's from this taboo on relocation that I've deduced a link between the species' tropism and its dichogamy. If the plants grow toward each other for the purpose of pollination, then perhaps their fluctuation in sex is just another change in the direction of a stimulus. Better not to interfere with whatever process enables each plant to seek out another.

I move on to an aisle of more mature plants, some of them still flowering and others with their petals fallen off, seeds almost ready to be retrieved. I pull off my glove by the fingers and let the stamen of a flower just whisper against my palm. Then I take a plant perhaps ready to harvest in hand. Seed pods protrude from the end of its stem—a cluster of vibrant green sacs joined together like the slices of an orange. Carefully, I run my bare thumb across their green circumference. Then I brush the raised seam where they join, and the sacs split open. A swarm of hard black seeds spills into my open palm.

An hour later, I'm in the shower. I turn on several faucets at once and fill the space with steam. Air whirs through the vent in the ceiling. In fly the men's voices, one at a time, steady, synonymous. Then the woman's voice, pitched, theatrical, upending like a glass of water. I begin to touch myself. I know I can't finish standing, so I get on my hands and knees on the tiled floor. I'm being loud. My voice presses against the other voices. It isn't enough. I flatten my cheek against the tile—my shoulders against the tile—the water is burning at my back. I lock my arms together and clasp my hands together into a hard fist and push and push until my eyes flame over with brilliant and colored light.

SOME DISASTER HAS happened. The plants have all turned male and none of them will turn back. None of them will bear seeds, like the descent of a plague. It takes us several weeks to confirm. We miss our reproduction targets entirely. We follow the instructions we receive by email. Prescribed adjustments to light, temperature, water, and air circulation fail to provoke any response. One thing is tried and then the next. At first, the perfunctory tone of the emails sets me at ease. But a month passes without improvement, and no higher power appears in person to investigate.

More than ever, I can't sleep. My balance is wrong. I trip on the edge of my bed at night and fall to my knees on the hard floor. My period, which was only ever a trickle, fails to come at all. I double and then triple the nutrient mix in my water tank, rearrange the troughs. The plants glisten with new vitality but remain barren.

Then they stop moving. The tropism vanishes. The greenhouse is static. The plants have stopped looking for each other.

Two months after the initial request for an increased harvest, I walk into the kitchen and find the men standing around the table with their glasses raised. Their bodies make dark shapes against the animation moving in silence on the television screen behind them. There is a general mood of triumph, a drink for me on the counter.

Our time at the facility is ending, John explains. He has received word. I think I read in him relief.

"The message mentioned you," John says.

I start.

"Well, it mentioned our report of the tropism as an alert to the impending change in the population, the end of the cycle. Apparently, this happens. It's rare, but it's happened before. After a period of increased tropic activity, reproduction halts. The population has selected a single plant to remain female and bear the reproductive burden for the whole, similar to a hive of bees serving a queen. The sole female plant can't be identified until it actually bears seeds, which can take anywhere from a week to a year. Regardless, the production of a single plant can't compare to the seed output of a normally distributed population. The contents of the entire greenhouse must be removed and the project begun again from scratch with new plants, raised from seeds, that have never interacted with each other."

"They're still alive," I say. "They haven't *spoiled*."

"Actually—for our purposes—they have."

In the morning, the message is there in my inbox, addressed to the team at large, none of us by name. We are to conclude operations. We will process any remaining seed pods from the previous reproductive cycle. We will digitize and submit the final round of notes. We will incinerate the remaining population of plants. We will incinerate the remaining population of plants, I read again. A hand is at my neck or must be for I begin breathing in short gasps.

I spend the week in a madness of work. The others won't be thorough, so I check each individual plant myself, labor in the greenhouse all day, and dream of flames at night. The men, their release in sight, descend into merriment. Dinners, they grin across the table. On Sunday, our meal over, I stride into the shower room, don't take off my clothes, just turn on a few of the faucets and stand next to the air vent. Soon, the voices reach me.

I'm back in the hallway. White lights blister. They're never off. The sounds of the men's conversation dim, barely audible through the thick facility walls. I can't hear the woman moaning until my ear is pressed against the door, my hand on the handle. Maybe I just want to see her face.

I fling the door open. The men are where I knew they'd be, sitting in their same seats, their chairs drawn flush against the table. None of their hands are immediately visible. But on the television screen: an image of a single white flower bisected. The flower's female organ, usually hidden within its white petals, blazes orange and furious against a black background. The grasping fingers of the stigma rest on the pillar-like style that widens at the base into the flower's ovary. Cut in half, the organ's tiny, flame-colored ovules arranged in twin lines are visible. They would have developed into seeds. Left in the dirt, they would have grown into flowers.

Hardly ten seconds have passed. The screen goes black,

someone forcefully yanking out the cord. But the white and orange of the flower were so intense, for a moment its image burns against my eyes in the new dark. They must have taken the picture here, but we aren't allowed to bring cameras of any kind into the facility. Even our phones are the old-fashioned kind, without lenses. They must have cut the flower open themselves. The woman's voice, I realize, has also vanished. We all look at each other in the dark.

I TELL MY mother I'm coming home and stomach her transparent glee. I include my resignation in my weekly report. Unwilling to ask John to deliver the message for me, I have no other means to tell anybody. I receive a response almost immediately: a car will be waiting to remove me from the facility on the date I've given, a precautionary quarantine to follow. I receive neither commendation for my work here nor acknowledgment that I'm breaking my contract.

I spend my last night in the greenhouse, slip back in before the door locks at seven. I remove my hood and the rest of my protective gear, fold them neatly, and carry them over my arm. I want to walk through the room like a garden. Slowly, I begin a pilgrimage up and down the five aisles, almost three miles of plants. Without my suit, I can feel the artificial wind sweeping gently through the room, hear the plants' tender jostling. Their leaves ruffle and sigh. And the smell—for once I can really smell the flowers' subtle fragrance. It accumulates as I walk, verdant and heady.

I find my way to the center of the greenhouse and lie down on the ground. The plants loom above me. Some faraway part of my mind revolts against the knowledge of what will happen to this place, but I'm so tired. Leaves whisper contently above me. White heads nod. For once, sleep feels possible. My body grows heavy; my eyes flutter; I drop into warm darkness.

I chose to keep a child once, when she was just a rhythm beneath my hand. In sleep, at last I allow for the enormity of loving that has taken root in me, love for someone who only promised to exist.

I wake feeling whole, entire, a new integrity in my body. I blink into darkness, a moment passing before I understand where the light has gone. While I slept, the plants bent across the aisle above, enclosing me in a warm, green shadow. Several white flowers dangle just above my face. I take one by the stem. The whole plant looks swollen. Its white flowering head droops heavily. Its stamens, usually hair thin, clasped by the mouth of the petals, are thick, laden with pollen. My breath scatters a cloud of orange. Sitting up, I get dressed in my suit. I duck beneath the bridge of stems and flowers and make my way into the open. I get to my feet, and my chest draws in sharp and quick.

Overnight, five thousand white flowers have turned to face me. The entire room of plants strains to reach me at its center. I walk and then begin to run. It takes several minutes to reach the exit. When at last I touch the door, I turn around and watch the flowers track my body, turn their heads in a massive wave like wind rippling through grass.

Several hours later, the men find me packing in my room. They've come to say goodbye. Each carries a black sealed bin in his arms, plants destined for incineration. The work begins today. I consider thanking them for agreeing to go on without me, but when I open my mouth, a white flower unfolds on my tongue. The air-conditioning kicks in. A fine orange substance drifts into the air. I see it glittering like a mist of electric rain.

"Nomi," one of them says.

Then they all fall down—asleep presumably.

Sonia Feldman is a writer from Cleveland, Ohio. She runs an email newsletter, *Sonia's Poem of the Week*, which reaches an audience of more than 1,500 readers every Friday. Her poetry has appeared or is forthcoming in journals like *The Missouri Review*, *The Southern Review*, and *Beloit Poetry Journal*. In 2022, Literary Cleveland named her a Breakthrough Writing Resident. She is at work on her first novel.

Editor's Note

Lisa Wartenberg Vélez's "What Is Ours" is a deeply observed and deeply disturbing examination of a family's silence and complicity in the face of a family member's crime. As we first read this story, we were immediately gripped by the intensity of the horror presented here. It made our skin crawl, not only in response to the crime, but because of the insidious way it is presented, with both the narrator and her family always approaching it obliquely, never willing to acknowledge its presence. It is there that the story especially shines, using small words and upsetting juxtapositions to build from the narrator's opening emotional paralysis to her final, yet ultimately misdirected, explosion.

The editors of *Nimrod International Journal* selected and published "What Is Ours" as a winner for *Nimrod*'s Francine Ringold Awards for New Writers, which celebrate the work of new writers with original, distinct voices, writers who are at the beginning of their careers but who we are sure will go on to achieve greater literary success and share many more unique stories. Lisa Wartenberg Vélez is just this kind of author, and "What Is Ours" is a remarkable example of this kind of story.

Eilis O'Neal, Editor in Chief
Nimrod International Journal of Prose and Poetry

What Is Ours

Lisa Wartenberg Vélez

ONCE UPON A TIME THERE WAS A LITTLE GIRL LOST *in the woods. She foraged for berries with which to heal her mother's lungs, until she fell and scraped her knee, old shoes ruined in mud. Just a little blood, a little mud, a voice said. She looked up and saw a wolf with eyes the color of oranges.*

AT MY GRANDMOTHER'S APARTMENT, Yessica serves us thick buñuelos, cured meats, pâté, European cheeses, blackberry jam, and a spread of cookies and freshens our drinks. It's funny. This is the food of celebration.

My five-year-old cousin says she wants a story. From my lap, she reaches for the bottled Coca-Cola, and her mother, my mother's sister, flicks her hand away and says Ah-ah—that'll ruin your teeth, then winks at me saying, Isn't that so? Reflexively I nod my head, letting specious concern widen my eyes at little Sofi. The girl retreats back onto my lap and loops her fingers into my rose-gold hoops. After my aunt and I trade a quick collusive smile, I notice my mother and grandmother lighting candles.

Tonight our family gathers to pray—for him, for our Uncle Mauricio, and for the girl too—to commemorate the one-year. A whole year. A Range Rover and a lost puppy—all the trite monstrosity of an *SVU* episode. Me, I don't pray—*I believe* is a thing we tell ourselves only to see our way out of the dark.

As people pluck food from trays and heap it onto plates, Sofi stacks her hand on mine and I note her dewy skin, the fleshiness, our square nail beds and brittle half-moons, the dimpled knuckles that will one day give way to joints jagged like mine.

Some jaunty music comes on and the room sparkles with Christmas. Yessica wipes crumbs from her apron and, at my grandmother's nod, she retires to her alcove in the kitchen.

THE WOLF PROMISED *the girl the way to the berries. She quivered, feet bare and sinking into a wet slop of earthworms. First you'll need new shoes, the wolf said, flashing the little girl a milky smile. You won't survive the forest otherwise.*

I SHOULD MENTION that in the fairy tale, I will not be playing the role of the girl. Imagine instead I am the trees and the birds and the ground the girl walks upon. I am the wind that blows and the dew dotting moss between hemlocks. For the time being, please forget I told you this and instead listen to yourself as you narrate the story. It is a real story. Talk to yourself like the rain.

LEILI DIED. NO.

Leili was murdered and so Leili died. Is dead. Her parents were too poor to experience a world beyond Bogotá, but by the time the police knocked on their door that morning they were well acquainted with its cruelty. Her body all pulped up like a wet map when it was found, ravaged as if by wildlings instead of people. No—one person, the newspapers said. I know him, I said. Am of him, I said.

Him.

But a person like that could never be known and, in this way, Uncle Mauri will never be known. A professor once said that to be fully known is to be fully alive. If this is true, then Uncle Mauricio has never fully existed. Will never. Flesh and blood, sure, he is that—but that is all he is, it turns out.

Little Leili was very real and alive and as expansive as the cosmos, they say, but is no longer. Yet we will never know her.

THE TWINS INCH up to the bar in oversized Fortnite and X-Men T-shirts and dare each other to spike their fizzing glasses of Postobón with decanted whiskey. Their snickers draw the attention of their father, who frowns at them from the bottom of his third Manhattan. Their father, who last year bought his mistress an abortion, according to my cousin Lina, Lina the lawyer with the live-in partner, Lina whose coming out almost cost her her inheritance, Lina who was smart enough to be out of town for this tonight. Truth is, I tried not to come, citing cramps and winter break projects, but I ultimately caved to the guilt. And I'll be gone in a few days, back into the fold of collegiate life across the ocean that so helps cast a mantle of illusion over this whole sordid mess. My stomach moans. Someone hands me a plate of cookies.

———

A FOOTHOLD. *The little girl asked the trees for a foothold when she ran into the white-fanged beast. That, or courage. Instead, the pine and balsam firs rattled free their loose leaves: they had seen this all before and relented to the density of their trunks, they swayed but did not break at the branches, did not screech, did not thunder themselves down in sacrifice.*

THEY WERE CLOSE, my mom and Uncle Mauri. And now they're close again, now that he's decided he is holy. My mom visits him every weekend and, separated by inch-thick glass, together they take to her rosary over sticky black receivers in the visitation room. This, the man whose Bible had once actually served as a doorstop, who once called priests rapists and punked them with off-the-wall confessions, who snuck booze into Mass and let me have some when I was twelve. This, the man whose horrors we gather around today.

THE LITTLE GIRL *looked around. Home was somewhere but no-where she could see beyond the trunks. No sounds but birds and the shud-dering of leaves and the pulsing of her heart.*

SOFI TUGS AT my collar and whispers. No, she says. She wants to know what really happened to the little girl that's gone. My brain spins.

Before I can respond my mother's sister says to me, Mauricio prays now, and she pulls at the lean golden cross that hangs on a chain above her collarbone. A mercy, she says. She looks at me expectantly. A silence lingers as I note the purple-gray fatigue ringing her eyes.

Across the room my mother breaks a wooden cocktail fork. She does not notice that it splinters and drops at her feet. My grandmother sits beside her in a tufted armchair and rises. She then lengthens her back and announces to the room, Perhaps this was all a blessing in disguise. It made him closer to God, she says. I peel flakes off my lips. My mom looks at my grandmother and—there is a pause before my mother nods. Behind them, fire laps into the throat of the chimney, rain pelts at the windows, air funnels out of the room, yet something bordering on joy ripples through the space and I watch each of my dozen or so relatives be swept up by it. Some hold hands. Even the twins seem arrested by this moment. They all look at my grandmother. My mom cries but I'm not sure who the tears are for.

I push against the weight of the air. A dead girl: a blessing in disguise.

We settle into silence, hands in our laps. I drink too much wine.

THE TREES STOOD *tall professing their sorrow but that is all they did. Birds towered high and, as the girl took the wolf's outstretched claws, they observed the sun. The girl marked her path with a long red ribbon from her cape, which didn't stand a chance against the wind.*

And—well, we know how this story ends.

———

MY EYES SETTLE on the marble table to my right. Its thick cold slab bears photos of Mauricio spanning his forty-odd years, not unlike an altar: the bonnets and the baby rolls and the Batman costume, the pimples and the study abroad, the opulent condos and the parties, and the smile blurs, the skin leathers, the eyes dull as the years wear on. How much more tragedy lurks along my uncle's dark edges, I am left to wonder. I recognize myself with him amid a fit of giggles, a mess of curls in a gum-pink shirt. Me and Mercedes's girl—Clarita, was it?—hang at his sides in a gold-embellished frame. I look about thirteen; she, ten. I sink into the seams of plush leather. His fingers grip just below her breast line. I feel my face flush.

Growing up and until I went to college, I stayed with Uncle Mauri during the summers and played with his live-in maid's kids. All girls except Yolanda's boy. Even then, what single man warranted a live-in was beyond me.

He'd pick me up from El Dorado airport, sleeves rolled up. He'd regale me with stories from his travels while I mawed into a roadside hot dog heaped with pineapple relish. He always had stories, and local lore, and plans for us, for all of us: the mall burgers at El Corral, the tamale brunches in bed, the mani-pedis at the salon, the tickle bombs, the tennis bracelets—me and the maids' girls, seven maids in the last five years alone, some gone before I ever dropped in for the summer. I don't even miss him. Or if I do, not him him—I miss the version of him I believed in for so long. I miss believing that person exists. Like, one July, during one of my sojourns here, my dog suddenly died back at home and I couldn't get out of bed. Couldn't eat, couldn't sleep. Mauricio began volunteering at a pet shelter and made me come with him, baited me out of bed with crêpes and coffee and a photo of a fluffy mutt named Pibe, and I had registered this then as the nicest thing anyone had ever done for me—wrote my goddamn college entrance essay about this.

I would throw it all away if I could, I would, the time with him—or, this him that is really not. Because if it weren't for me, the girls wouldn't have been allowed in the guest room, or the living room, or my bathtub to play ponies. If it weren't for me, some of them would have been spared. I wish knowing that made it any easier to bear. Because it was right there in front of me, of us, ten, fifteen years ago it was there, all those summers at his duplex: attention that bordered on obsessive, his largesse, a fiery smile snuffed out by the quick blaze of his inflexibility. Mercedes, Mariana, Yesenia, all of them: before long they were eyes down, guards up, girls close, each of them.

Most of our games took place when groceries or other errands rendered us alone with him in the apartment. Me and Socorro's girl, Yanira, who loved to dance salsa, who knew every lyric to Carlos Vives. We'd break out into song, or play supermodel, or this one time he had us play dog, where she was my pet and I walked her around the apartment tethered to a scarf. Or, how I never questioned that an eight-year-old needs help in the shower. Or, how one other summer I remember that I thought I saw a shadow creep past the garret in the kitchen. I told him the next day I'd seen a monster but he promised me it was just a trick of the eyes and that monsters weren't real and that if they were he'd be there to save me from them. And the bite marks I found on Clarita's shoulder—it took me twelve years to realize that no craning of the neck would ever allow her to do that to herself.

And me. Well, I suppose every fishhook needs bait.

———

IF IT HADN'T been for the doorman they would've probably never found him out. At least not this time, this time with Leili.

Of course there had been others.

You don't just one day decide to steal your sister's car, drive out to the poorest part of Bogotá, and then kidnap, drug, and brutalize a child before stuffing her into the pockets of an outdoor hot tub—wrenching open its side cabinet, gutting plumbing encased by its plastic shell, making room for her, all parts of her, gathering inky hair into a mound, shoving her inside, knocking against bone, before rinsing and bleaching, before scrubbing and closing, before drawing over the cover and zipping it up. Before all that. No, you build up to that. You blur those boundaries, erode their edges bit by bit, let them get soft, get crumbly, get gone—first the drugs, for you; then the want, for them; then the decision to act on the want, for that specific want. Then the realization that maybe, just maybe, you could get away with acting on it.

So you do. And you can. A little thing, you think, until that thing is no longer enough. Until, again, you need more. For your gums to numb and your blood to boil and your shit to be hot and you to feel alive.

Or until the brand-new, not-in-on-it doorman waves you in as you lead a wobbling child into your too-big, too-bare luxury apartment you only now visit on the weekends.

BACK TO THE wolf and the trees. There's something I forgot in there.

In the forest with the magical berries, leather work boots crushed fallen leaves. The Huntsman. He followed the wolf and the little girl a mountain's length until they neared a cabin near a ravine.

YESSICA REENTERS WITH a tray of tinto and chamomile. How she, or anyone, still works for this family defies logic. Survival, I suppose, has sharper teeth than that.

Our eyes meet and shift with the friction of reluctant understanding. I thumb the cookie on my plate into crumbs. She used to change my diapers and now I can't even look her in the eye. They lived on the same street, she and Leili's mother, at the time anyway, who knows—Yessica and I don't talk anymore. I can't bring myself to small talk or real talk, so instead I scroll my phone or look at the ceiling, feigning interest in the shadows, in the Baroque crown molding, until she leaves the room and I've failed again in a new way. Sometimes I'll look my uncle up and am inevitably met with the photo of Leili's mother clutching at her chest, as if it didn't already flashbulb into my mind's eye over and over—the candlelight vigils, the posters, the white roses—it's like a goddamn movie. And of course Yessica knows all about it. The case still makes the papers.

PEERING THROUGH A *window the Huntsman saw the little girl in the cabin, the wolf spooning a mossy soup into her mouth.*

MY AUNT IS talking. Something still about mercy. About rugged paths and darkness, about finding your way to a reckoning

with God, about salvation and redemption and how perhaps this
was Uncle Mauri's own journey to the holy.

What is ours: hands worn stiff from clutching at a lie; a heavy
head and a cut tongue; the shame of loving a monster.

Yessica drops the napkins, and no one helps. Not even me. Because I can't move. Instead my throat tightens, my mouth awash
with nausea. There is such a danger here.

A little girl dead: the price of a man's atonement. I think about
Leili's family somewhere across the city in their tin-roofed home,
clinging to each other, to their memories of their little girl gone,
dead, murdered, brutalized, disposed of like a crumpled-up map
and wedged into the sides of a Jacuzzi tub. No one has said her
name tonight. Not once. It is a thing we sit with and refuse to look
at, that grows larger the longer we sit, and now there is no room
for us to breathe. This is who we are. This is who we choose to be.
I look at my mother and see his eyes. I look at my mother and see
myself in her face. My heart hammers against my rib cage: I am my
blood, I am my blood, I am my blood. I cannot speak. The room
careens. I excuse myself, but before I can stand I vomit on my skirt.

THE HUNTSMAN ROLLED *up his sleeves and drew an arrow from
his quiver. He inhaled sharply.*

I CHANGE INTO my aunt's yoga pants and Yessica has already
cleaned up my mess. My little cousin tinkers around the wet spot at
my feet and climbs back onto my lap. She'll be Leili's age next year.
Bogotá has a boogeyman, they said to me at her age. These are not

the stories I want to tell Sofi. He meanders through streets looking for loitering children. I had been warned about leaving the court-yard within our complex or risk being scooped up into a satchel and eaten alive by this monster. The inevitability of this always struck me, effecting its intended terror, festering in my child's mind. The monster, they told me, was elsewhere.

AT THE SIGHT *of the man, the wolf bolted closed the wooden door. The Huntsman smiled.*

THE PHONE RINGS and Yessica answers. She passes the phone to my grandmother, who, phone to ear, is silent and performs lis-tening for us, eyes darting from side to side—a prerecorded mes-sage, it seems, at the end of which she says, Sí, acepto.

It's him.

THE WOLF RAN *to the window and slid shut the curtains. He or-dered the girl to hide under the cot as the Huntsman fumbled with the doorknob.*

MY GRANDMOTHER SETS down the receiver and puts him on speakerphone. Clutching at her rosary and her Kleenex with trem-bling hands, she pleads to her God for the redemption of Un-cle Mauri's soul. One by one each relative takes turns shouting pleasantries and God-talk into the mouthpiece, each exaltation like a drum in a dirge.

¡La gloria del Señor!

¡Dios me lo bendiga, mijito!

¡Él sabe como hace sus cosas!

There's a lot of thanking the glory of God. This all then, I presume, is such glory manifest. I wonder which among us would have the gall to say that in front of Leili's family.

"¿Está Sofi por ahí?" Mauricio says. Put Sofi on the line. I imagine his hairy knuckles clutching at the receiver, the thick scar along his index finger from that boating accident in Cartagena.

"Saludalo," her mother mouths at her. Say hi. She arches her brows for emphasis, to convey that she really means it, young lady.

My hands pulse, soften with sweat. I want to hold her. I want to whisper, You don't have to talk to him if you don't want to—but everyone is looking. I swish my wine instead.

Sofi wiggles off my lap and contorts her lips. As her mother waves her forward, she patters bare feet closer to the phone. The girl looks out from the corner of her eyes and breaks with timidness through a soft hello.

The room *awws*.

THE HUNTSMAN KICKED open the door to the wolf's cabin. The little girl cried from beneath the cot as the wolf ran into the depths of the forest leaving the Huntsman and the girl alone.

The Huntsman pulled knotted fingers against the bowstring, piercing the little girl's thigh. She shrieked, then grew heavy with sleep. The

Huntsman scooped up her limp body and laid it out on the kitchen table.
He shut the door.

IT'S MY TURN to speak. My mouth is bone-dry, my hands rattle. Something blurts out of me and before I realize, I am suddenly ensnared by a dozen gaping faces. I am no longer sitting, I am rising. Am no longer watching, I am snatching my purse. I step outside into the bleary Bogotá night, and as I fish for my phone a car splashes water onto my coat. Umbrella-shadowed faces dash past and alongside me on the sidewalk, foregrounding my aunt's Range Rover parked dead on flattened tires. The last car Leili ever got into. A car I rode in. The car the police didn't have any use for anymore and the world itself didn't know what to do with.

A man bumps against me. "¿Qué le pasa?" he says in a cigarillo voice. What's my problem? he wants to know. I rebound, curl my hand like a claw, but we disband—his left, my left—and as I shuffle closer toward traffic, I stumble against brick edging around a thick eucalyptus. My hands blush from the concrete and I push up to sit, the lip of my moss-green coat sullied in a puddle. I look back at the gilded iron door of the building. Then I see the Range Rover still heavy against the asphalt. The rain stings my eyes. I dig into the mulch. I draw my chin up like an arrow in the sky. I run, brick in hand. Against my face the glass bursts, a constellation of rage, its shards glittering at my feet.

Lisa Wartenberg Vélez is a writer of fiction who split her childhood between South Florida and Colombia. Her work has received support from Bread Loaf, Tin House, and Kenyon Review 2022 Writers Workshops. She received her MFA ('23) in fiction from University of Houston CWP. She is at work on her first novel. With love to Bennett, Rob, Mamá, Papá, Milo, and all of her family.

About the Judges

VENITA BLACKBURN's works have appeared in *The Atlantic*, thenewyorker.com, *Harper's*, *Ploughshares*, *McSweeney's*, *The Paris Review*, and others. She received the Prairie Schooner book prize in fiction for her collected stories, *Black Jesus and Other Superheroes*, in 2017. She is founder of the literary nonprofit Live, Write (livewriteworkshop.com), which provides free creative writing workshops for communities of color. Blackburn's second collection of stories is *How to Wrestle a Girl*, 2021, finalist for a Lambda Literary Prize. She is an Associate Professor of creative writing at California State University, Fresno.

RICHARD CHIEM is the author of *You Private Person* (Sorry House Classics, 2017) and the novel *King of Joy* (Soft Skull, 2019), which was longlisted for the 2020 PEN Open Book Award. He was named a 2019 Writer to Watch by the *Los Angeles Times*. *You Private Person* was named one of *Publishers Weekly*'s 10 Essential Books of the American West. He has taught at Hugo House and Catapult. He lives in Seattle.

DANTIEL W. MONIZ is the recipient of a National Book Foundation "5 Under 35" Award, a Pushcart Prize, a MacDowell Fellowship, and the Alice Hoffman Prize for Fiction. Her debut collection, *Milk Blood Heat*, is the winner of a Florida Book Award and was a finalist for the PEN/Jean Stein Award, the PEN/Robert W. Bingham Prize, and the New York Public Library Young Lions Fiction Award, as well as longlisted for the Dylan Thomas Prize.

Her writing has appeared in *The Paris Review, Harper's Bazaar, American Short Fiction, Tin House,* and elsewhere. Moniz is an assistant professor at the University of Wisconsin-Madison, where she teaches fiction.

About the PEN/Robert J. Dau Short Story Prize for Emerging Writers

The PEN/Robert J. Dau Short Story Prize for Emerging Writers recognizes twelve fiction writers for a debut short story published in a print or online literary magazine. The annual award was offered for the first time during PEN America's 2017 literary awards cycle.

The twelve winning stories are selected by a committee of three judges. The writers of the stories each receive a $2,000 cash prize and are honored at the annual PEN America Literary Awards Ceremony in New York City. Every year, Catapult publishes the winning stories in *Best Debut Short Stories: The PEN America Dau Prize.*

This award is generously supported by the family of the late Robert J. Dau, whose commitment to the literary arts has made him a fitting namesake for this career-launching prize. Mr. Dau was born and raised in Petoskey, a city in Northern Michigan in close proximity to Walloon Lake, where Ernest Hemingway had spent his summers as a young boy and which serves as the backdrop for Hemingway's *The Torrents of Spring.* Petoskey is also known for being where Hemingway determined that he would commit to becoming a writer. This proximity to literary history ignited the Dau family's interest in promoting emerging voices in fiction and spotlighting the next great fiction writers.

List of Participating Publications

PEN America and Catapult gratefully acknowledge the following publications, which published debut fiction in 2022 and submitted work for consideration to the PEN/Robert J. Dau Short Story Prize.

Adi Magazine

Alaska Quarterly Review

American Short Fiction

Apparition Literary Magazine

Apricity Magazine

The AutoEthnographer

Baltimore Review

Bellevue Literary Review

Belmont Story Review

Bennington Review

Big Bend Literary Magazine

The Bitchin' Kitsch

Blackbird: an online journal of literature and the arts

CALYX Journal

CARVE

Catamaran Literary Reader

Chicago Quarterly Review

The Cincinnati Review

Cloaca Mag

Cold Mountain Review

The Common

CRAFT
Do Not Research
Driftwood Press
Epiphany
failbetter
Fairy Tale Review
Five Points
Fleas on the Dog
Foglifter
The Gettysburg Review
Girls Right the World
Granta
The Gravity of the Thing
Hawai`i Pacific Review
HEAT
Humber Literary Review Spotlight
Hypertext Magazine
Kelp Journal
The Kenyon Review
Litro
Longleaf Review
MER – Mom Egg Review
Michigan Quarterly Review
Moot Point Magazine
The Moth
Mount Hope
the museum of americana
The Mustard Review
Narrative

Nimrod International Journal of Prose and Poetry

NUNUM

Obsidian: Literature & Arts in the African Diaspora

Ocean State Review

The Offing

One Story

Oxford Review of Books

Peatsmoke Journal

Pigeon Pages

Ploughshares

Porter House Review

Potato Soup Journal

PRISM international

Salt Hill

sinθ / Sine Theta Magazine

Solarpunk Magazine

Solstice: A Magazine of Diverse Voices

Southeast Review

Split Lip Magazine

Stanchion

Stonecoast Review

Subnivean

The Summerset Review

Thanatos Review

Tint Journal

The Unconventional Courier

Waxwing

West Trade Review

Witness

Permissions

PEN America stands at the intersection of literature and human rights to protect open expression in the United States and worldwide. The organization champions the freedom to write, recognizing the power of the word to transform the world. Its mission is to unite writers and their allies to celebrate creative expression and defend the liberties that make it possible. Learn more at pen.org.